Prologue

Organon

Peace breeds insecurity. Subterfuge replaces violence, and alliances are forged in chains of leverage.

The Oracle: The Book of Lore.

From the beginning, The First Oracle of the Veil ruled with benevolence over Organon. The Oracle was the sole emissary to a mystic power known as the Veil, a deep and unrelenting force that lived deep beneath the ancient city of Elysian. In return for prosperity, she demanded unwavering faith, promising peace, and bounty to all those who followed her.

But, as with all devotion, faith wavered, and as the first epoch came to an end, after nearly a thousand cycles of providence, her people grew restless in their worship.

Fearing her fall, the Oracle warned the righteous against their blasphemy, warning her people with a prophecy of the storm to come.

Yet her desperate threats fell on deaf ears, betrayal was in the air.

It was the Day of Convergence on the Annulum calendar, celebrating the ascension of the Oracle and her reign over Organon. Miya and Minor met in the sky, plunging the city's waning light into a brief but total darkness. As the moons parted on this most sacred day, the end of the annual Scorch was marked with the beginning of Dampfall, the season of rains.

The cobbled streets of Elysium were heavily crowded as the rains descended. Cityfolk fell in their thousands upon the Oracle's temple, their usual reverence plagued with doubt and anger.

As twilight took hold, lanterns slowly glowed into view across the throng of people. This day, unlike so many others, rang with the seed of discontent that had been newly sown. The boldest marched to the gates with protest and vigour in their hearts. Fear set in behind the gilded arches, as she watched with a heavy heart, her empire was crumbling before her eyes. Despite a millennia of servitude and harmony, her people had revolted against her grace. In a sudden fit of rage, the Oracle fled to the deepest depths of Elysium to fulfil her prophecy and reached into the Veil to awaken the storm that lay eagerly at in its heart.

The Veil was breached.

From it the Veilstorm, a great beast over two hundred feet wide and a thousand needle sharp teeth, came crashing through the temple, tearing through its majestic columns and arches like an axe through balsa. All was lost in its gaping jaws. The beast struck with such resounding force that Organon, over a thousand leagues wide, was split in two, forever carving the continent asunder. Elysium's destruction was complete, the screams of the unfaithful eternally swallowed into the void as the sea poured into the chasm that the beast behind as it returned to the depths.

Those who survived the cataclysm begged for redemption, for her providence but it would be a hundred cycles until hope would return to Organon.

More cycles passed, until the Oracle and the Veilstorm fell into myth and legend. As the sea dividing

Organon remained, a lasting fear the Veil's unknown power survived among those who would come to rebuild civilisation in its shadow.

To the west, the new continent of Aridus now lay bare, its rolling hills scorched by an oppressive sun. But in time the city of Alkpine sprang into life, where a chosen few would come to rule. Led by the Imperator, Lysander of Alkpine, his council ruled with meritocratic law, favouring proficiency over omnipotence.

Despite Alkpine's success, the Veil's turbulent waters would claim the lives any who dared to venture east by sea. The Veil remained impassable but for a perilous journey across the Reach among the northern shoals.

While Alkpine grew in isolation, dreamers in the east whispered of a return to providence, waiting on the Oracle's return to reunite the world. Umidus was a land of great contrast, with jagged peaks cutting through its centre. In the north-west, the lush forest of Oakston thrived, with verdant plains and sandy dunes reaching out into the south. Beyond the great ridge, the terrain shifted—the verdant landscape gave way to Kreig, where rocky flats were scarred by lonely mountains with hidden secrets.

In the Umidus plains, Tifern emerged as a new power. Claiming descendance from the First Oracle, Calliope leveraged her political prowess to declare Tifern a Caliphate, granting her dominion across the continent. With calculated precision and divine blessing, she ensured Tifern's prosperity. Yet some whispered of a false prophet, plotting her demise.

Fiercely cunning, Calliope used her influence to seek a path across the Veil, and when a source was found, she moved quickly to control it. She anointed Steers to traverse the perilous waters, using a hidden secret to smooth their journey, allowing the trade of both resource and commodity between the continents. For Alkpine, the Veil remained impassable, leading to a dependence on their eastern neighbours.

South of Tifern, among the craters and burnt hues of the Heuranon desert, hid the truth behind Calliope's secret, taenite. Haru, Prince of Dunes, who lorded over this precious metal, sought his own power, plotting quietly beneath the Heurn mountains, waiting for the moment to strike.

Chapter One

The Moons Rise

True freedom is not found by removing bondage,

but by measuring the weight of it.

Alleric, Commander of Swords: The Path of the

Paladin

Barrow Harbour sat high on the western coast of Umidus, heavy with a mix of salt and pitch in the air. The Steerport, a grand rotunda of sandstone and slate dominated the skyline. The building served as the bustling northern hub for Tifern's merchants and officials, marking the boundary of their influence on the continent.

    Pressed tightly against the stone walls, a sprawl of buildings and shacks spilled out onto city's boardwalks and crossroads, weighed down with the great burden of ships tied-up for deepnight, stole the last late glow of the setting sun which stretched across the water. Miya and Minor, cast a shallow light on the alcoves and hidden alleys beneath the Steerport's gaze.

As Miya climbed every higher above her sibling, Berwick stared out towards the Veil. There was a terrible beauty among its chaos, the moonlight cast its sheen over the moving waters. Quiet contemplation was etched across his soft round features. He felt small while watching the chopping waves ebb and flow, like the ripples from a stone, cast into the sea. He was soothed by a cooling breeze, bumps raising across his skin, gently caressing after the muggy heat of the first day of Dampfall.

His thoughts turned to his father, once Astra Paladin, Aleric had commanded over a thousand swords, but when Calliope ascended, she demanded absolute control among her ranks. She reshaped the Paladin into her own private army, the swords that once served the former king now bent to her divine will. Those who wouldn't submit were stripped of their honour. She purged those loyal to her father, replacing them with weaker minds who would not question her authority and grace.

The Paladin were at the highest echelon of society, second only to the King's Council. They trained from an early age in both statecraft and war, their swordsmanship and sacred taenite weapons unmatched in the world. Yet, Alleric fell from grace now keeping to a nomadic life on the fringes of Tifern control.

Berwick shared his father's salt-flecked, dark hair, but his elder brother Godric inherited the majority of his father's looks and stature. Aleric's best days were behind him, and he vicariously lived through his eldest son. At twenty-two, Godric was infuriatingly handsome, and talented in every pursuit.

Both sons were trained in the Path of the Paladin, yet Berwick, favouring tactics over brawn, could only watch with envy as his brother grew into the shape of their father. At fourteen, Berwick still had many years ahead of him, but the thought of always being overshadowed gnawed at him. He had tried to accept his place in the family but deep down, he still harboured a flicker of defiance, a quiet hope that one day, his own talents might be enough. Aleric rarely said it outright, but Berwick could feel the weight of his father's silent expectations, hanging over him like the sword he could never truly wield.

As he watched over to Veil, the air comforted Berwick, but soon he grew tired of the ever-crashing ocean. Both moons now hung high overhead, the day had been long, the salt spray began to ache his weary eyes. Their father had followed a lead in the docks, seeking information on the Oracles ascension but had yet to return.

"What's bothering you Wick?" Godric smiled, his eyes watching his brother.

Berwick's brow deepened, "Father should be back by now, what's taking him so long?"

"I'm sure it's nothing, should we head back to the Hollow? I caught a cony this morning, we can roast with some wild garlic,"

"Yes, fine" Berwick answered, not completely convinced.

Patrols often went looking for trouble, and the pair had learnt the art of dancing through the shadows to avoid unwanted attention, "Come on, before Minor sets and we're left to scamper in the dark," his woven cloak swaying in the breeze.

The pair quickly moved through to the outskirts of Barrow. Like cats, they scampered with an elegant grace, easily hurdling the hubbub of the stone, mortar, and timber. As night darkened, the warm glow of oil lamps guided them to the quietening streets. The gate itself was heavily guarded, only the swift patter of street-rats stood between the ironclad warriors who stood vigil over the sandstone walls. "Should we join the late arrivals, Godric?" Berwick asked, observing the queue of traders hoping to exit through the gate. "You remember how that went last time?" Godrick answered, "not a chance! Look, that grate, can you squeeze through?" The thick stone walls were made without flaw, but like thieves in the night, they crept through the tall grass to a well-worn water channel in the wall. It was shallow, a light trickle flowing through the watergate.

"It will be tight Godric, let's go…" the gate easily gave way, and both boys snuck through into the night.

Once out of the harbour, their pace slowed. Beads of sweat began to cover Berwick, his breath heavy with the rush of adrenaline coursing through his body. As they reached out into the blackness, they found the steady stream that would lead them to their rest stop. A tidy hollow, lightly decorated with brush and reeds, it was a welcome sight for weary travellers in need of rest. Heavy from the journey, the boys quickly settled into a well-rehearsed routine, water, firewood, dinner, until finally they settled down for the night. They did not know it, but as Aleric approached in haste.

Chapter Two

Duty

To know your enemy, one must first know oneself.

It is the only path to true power.

Qadi, Scrollmaster to Lysander, The Veil's

Whisper

Seated high above the keep, within the dolomite halls of the Citadel, Poppy's chamber was a circular room of rich mahogany and soft plush carpet. Her hand gently rested against a writing desk, an empty gaze sweeping across the great city below her. Her father, the Imperator, had summoned her once again. *Must he persist with this betrothal?!* she thought, worry clinging to her delicate features.

As she thought on the arrangement, Poppy's stomach tightened.

This wasn't what she wanted, but duty weighed heavily on her shoulders. It was more than an alliance—but a calculated move to solidify ties between Alkpine and

Oakston, securing a vital trade partner in a move against the Oracle. Her father's position was growing untenable after the duty imposed by Tifern steadily increased, yet the thought of being trapped in a political contract gnawed at her.

She set down the parchment, a deep red seal gleaming in the fading light, as she ran a delicate hand through her tawny hair. Letting out a long sigh, she pushed away from her perch. The setting sun cast a pink hue over the limestone walls, beautifully complementing the slate roofs of the city below. Pulling on a golden robe, she summoned the servants to get ready "A hard day lies ahead," she murmured, her thoughts carrying the weight of trepidation.

Alkpine was a marvel of engineering. The Citadel towered over the bustling streets below, its shadow stretching across the city. Only the Cenotaph, standing at the city's heart, interrupted the view. A thick limestone wall encircled the city, its pale surface gleaming faintly under the midday sun. Iron gates barred entry from the barren wastes beyond, where dust devils twisted across the cracked earth. The Clearwater, once flowing through the heart of Alkpine, now circled the city's walls, feeding the fortified wharf that stretched into the Veil below. At the docks, ships piloted by Steers crowded the water, their sails set toward the Veil, with the Torch guiding their passage through its treacherous waves.

Her piercing blue eyes traced the distant horizon. She would miss the sight before her, but as a light wind carried the city's familiar scent into her chambers, she smirked. "Not the smell," she thought.

After the fussing had finished, Poppy stood before the looking glass, a tall yet graceful princess staring back. Wrapped in an olive-green traveling cloak—practical, yet elegant—her hair was woven delicately and draped over the hood. The leather riding boots gave her a sense of height, adding an air of authority to match her strong will. "I will not falter," she told herself. "They will not see my fear." Determination gleamed in her eyes. With a final, approving glance, she led her attendants down the winding stairs toward the great oak doors of the throne room, though a nervous fluttering still lingered in her mind.

The doors swung open before her, the air thick with anticipation. The room's towering ceilings, adorned with majestic arches and tapestries, seemed to press down on her. A long red carpet muted the soft glow of the tiled floor, guiding her toward the raised platform where her father sat. Her footsteps echoed loudly in the vast space, stone columns looming with each step. This sacred hall, designed to intimidate all who entered, made this feel like the longest walk of her life.

At the dais, her father, Lysander, looked down upon her. A man of great stature, his crown of silver sat awkwardly atop a mop of auburn hair streaked with grey, matched by a mid-length beard that lent him an air of wisdom and power. Yet sorrow clouded his eyes. As the princess approached, he dipped his gaze, finding solace in the floor instead of meeting her approach.

Beside the Imperator stood Vizier Ren, a wiry figure whose thin, cruel smile lingered in the air as he whispered into Lysander's ear. His presence, heavy with unchecked ambition, filled the room. Seated at the modest benches of the council, Armsmaster Varang, Coinmaster Ryo, Lawmaster Qadi, and Scrollmaster Hoplite watched in silent judgment.

An awkward silence cut the air, only the casual shuffle of robes could be heard above her heartbeat – stepping away casually from the throne, the Vizier broke the tension as he stepped down from the dais.

"Finally princess, you are here – are you ready to tell us your decision?" He used a resounding voice that heralded the room, reverberating through every alcove and statue that lined the walls.

"You have made clear to me, Vizier, the decision is not mine to argue – but I will go freely, I am prisoner here after all." She replied, a steady strength in her reply, hiding the nervous flutter she felt.

"Dear Poppy," her father said softly, "I do not wish to see you like this, we must all do our part to secure this realm. For too long we have been subjected to the whims of that damned Oracle and her authority over the sea. Enough I say, let us carve out our own future, I beg you."

There was emotion in his voice, a pleading, begging her to accept this fate with grace, but she could not. If she were being sent away, across the Veil, it would not be with good grace. "Oh Father, how you sit there – comfortable with the plans of your council, what would my mother say? How they control your narrative brings sadness to my heart. I will go to Oakston and secure this pact you have made, but do not expect me to pretend that this is what I want. Sold to some foreign prince like gold for barter. I will not submit to your vanity. I pray that when I leave this place, you remember what held this Imperium together. It was not the whispered conspiring of academics, but a balance of love and desire to do good." As she finished, her voice started to crack, tears formed, but would not yield, it made her eyes glisten in the dull light.

"I, I..." His lips parted as if to speak, but only a sigh escaped. His hands fell to the arms of his throne, in resignation. "Your mother was chosen, just as you are now.

That is how our society thrives, Poppy. You, and one day your child, represent the last of our blood to lead this Imperium. Before a new line is chosen."

"Excellent," Ren announced, his pointed hands clasped together in bitter unison as a wry smile crept across his face. There was an energy to his voice that surprised Lysander, why was he so desperate to remove her? The Imperator thought?

"The arrangements have been made. You are to leave immediately. Gather your things and attend the Royal Stables. Your litter awaits. Pack lightly—you have a long ride ahead. You can send for your things... once you're settled.." He said with a pause.

"I will not travel like some priced trinket," she argued, "ready my horse, who will escort me?"

"Why the Imperator's personal guard, of course" he replied questioningly.

With one last glace at her father, she turned and fled. That would be the last time she would ever see him.

Chapter Three

Night at The Hollow

Fear is the shadow we cannot outrun.

Alleric, Commander of Swords, The Path of the Paladin

Both moons had set, the night's blackness offset brilliantly by stars that flecked the sky with a soft, purple transcendence. The brothers lay in peaceful slumber, nestled neatly into the Hollow's tidy arrangement of branches and ferns, sheltered from the light patter of rain that hung in the air. A distant rumbling woke Berwick suddenly, his eyes wide and alert. He sat upright, turning to see Godric's sleep undisturbed by the sudden intrusion in the night. He watched for a moment, his brother's chest slowly moving in a gentle rhythm. The mat laid for their father sat empty, untouched. Berwick wondered where his father was. Something about his absence troubled him, though he couldn't pinpoint why.

The rumbling grew louder, like the steady drum of a song building to its crescendo. As Berwick stared into the dark, the rain biting at his stillness, a single light appeared down-river. The lone torch marched toward them, its pace quickening. Finally, Godric stirred.

"Wake up you fool!" he cried.

"What is it?" Godric grumbled, clearly unhappy with being woken.

"Look. Something is coming." He pointed towards the ominous light, carelessly flickering between the trees. His stomach tightened, and his breath quickened. A thousand thoughts began to spin into a tight web across his mind. Closer now, the drumming was quickly replaced with the loud rustle of heavy boots, crashing through the stream. They had crossed the ford.

"Is that..." Godric started, cut off by sudden realisation.

"Yes, it's father!" Berwick finished, "But... why is he running?."

"Wick, hide, I don't like this."

As he approached, sweat and dirt mucked across his strong brow, Berwick dove under cover.

"Run!"

A voice called out from the dark. Fear flickered across Godric's face as Aleric stumbled forward. More torches appeared on the horizon, drawing closer with each passing moment. Godric scrambled into the brush next to their campfire, pulling up his robe to secure his dignity. Beside him, an oak chest sat, inlaid with delicate metal trim, and secured by a clasp of iron. Atop, a leather scabbard called to him, and without thinking, he unsheathed a sword of unrivalled splendour. A mark of the Paladin, the taenite blade glistened against the starlight, bearing a thousand colours, almost glowing. He turned to face the oncoming hoard, a renewed strength flowing through his arm.

"No boy, you must flee – it's me they want!" Aleric croaked, a deep cuts now visible across his cheek, a red aglow against the torch.

Composed Godric stood his ground, fighting against the rain which now thundered down with a relentless might.

"Who are they, Father? Why are they coming?" Godric's voice remained steady, though his grip tightened on the sword.

"The Veil, they… they think the Paladin know the secret – it's not Tifern …Alk…"

Before he could finish, a black steel shaft, cruelly hooked at the end, broke through his chest. A final gasp escaped him. As he fell to his knees, the terror drained from his eyes. Alleric the Paladin was dead.

Berated by what he saw, the purest rage filled Godric. Without a second thought, he charged. But the approaching guard, was ready. Godric moved with the grace of a trained warrior, his blade flashing through the rain-soaked night. For a moment, it seemed, he might hold them back, each strike pushing them away. But the sheer numbers overwhelmed him, pressing in on all sides. His movements grew frantic, his strikes wild, until finally, the mob surrounded him completely.

Unable to breathe, Berwick clamped his hands over his ears, desperate to block out the clash of steel and thunder of hooves. There were too many, and despite gallant skill, Godric joined his father in the dirt, now a swamp of wet mud and grass, matted with bright red. Steeling a single glance, mutilated shapes gaped back through empty sockets. Berwick's body refused to move, frozen in time as his mind swirled between denial and horror. He wanted to scream, but no sound escaped his lips. His voice had been stolen, suffocated by the terror that gripped him, leaving him paralyzed by fear. All was lost.

Chapter Four

Desert Schemes

Beware, not of the snake in the grass, but the poison in the veins of the mouse.

Phalanx, First King of Dunes: Truth in the Sand

South of the Razors, deep within the pointed caves that lead into the Sakana delta, a length of polished ebony stretched across a dimly lit chamber. The edges of the table were delicately carved into the shape of the known world, rivers and mountains etched beautifully across its surface. A deep fissure ran through its centre, splitting the expanse in two.

Smoke curled through the air, as Haru sat at the table's head, resting lightly on over the Reach. His dark skin was draped in elegant silk, made for the desert's heat in mauve and gold trim. In contrast, the Vizer wore his usual black robe, a speared circle stitched across the front. Ren grinned eagerly at the man across from him, his face pale in the candlelight. Enjoying the awkward silence, Ren claimed a pewter chalice ahead of him filled with sour-red wine, taking a long draught to quench his thirst, until Haru broke the tension.

"How can you be so sure? If this fails... well, let's just say the cursed Oracle will tighten the noose around our necks for good." A nervous hand, decorated in shimmering metal, accompanied his deep, croaked voice. He moved to hover over the High Gardens, where Calliope has taken residence.

"Most certainly, my dear prince. I oversaw it myself. The princess has just reached the Cape of Bones. Tomorrow, she will arrive at Patron, where she will be safe—until the time is right. My most gracious Imperator knows nothing of our plans, all is as expected your grace."

As Prince of Dunes, Haru was no more than a proxy, serving at the Oracle's whim. His territory reached from coast to coast in the red southern desert, but Heurn had always lived in the shadow of Tifern's wealth and resource. But oppression slowly burns into hate, and his people grew tired of the levies and tax. Trade with Tiffern was becoming difficult to justify.

The Vizier paused for a moment, reading the man opposite. Haru's expression had filled with concern, his wide features lined with age, kept alive by the golden eyes of to the desert mountains. The pair sat in a small and empty room, dark with conspiracy, yet eyes watched in the shadows. As he thought on the Viziers words, the shadow moved to Haru's side, his concubine Ayume. Her sulking in the fringes had not gone unnoticed by Ren, and he wondered on her motives as the silence continued.

Haru wasn't built for conspiracy and had enjoyed many years on the throne of sand. Ayame however, was young, immeasurably beautiful, and intelligent. She used these advantages well, planting the intoxicating seeds of ambition in Haru's heart. A subtle pressure from her leading hand rested on his shoulder as if goading him into his reply. Her bright mind gleamed with possibility, a vision of greatness – stirring something in the prince that he couldn't deny.

"Caution by love, we must not play into the hands of the Alkpine Council." Her last words before entering the room.

Seeing his prince's hesitation, the Vizier noted how the balance of power had shifted in that moment, a brief smirk crept onto his face. His mind is fragile Ren thought.

"Fear not, my prince," Ren said smoothly. "She will only see what we allow her to see. Her powers do not reach into the minds of men—only the storm that she can't hope to control. All we must do now is wait."

Chapter Five

The Reach

The battlefield is a tumultuous place, won in the playful dance of strategy and timely fortune. The inner battleground is far more treacherous, where deep, unscalable caverns grow. Yet those who conquer their darkest depths will see that true victory lies within.

Qadi, Scrollmaster to Lysander: The Veil's Whisper

How anyone could survive that crossing is beyond me! Popelina's thoughts serving as light relief as she dragged herself up a grey mound out of the water, each step heavier than the last.

After six hours of relentless trudging, even her chaperones were worn thin. They had waded through the shallow reef, her riding boots barely protecting her from the sharp bite of shoals and rocks that snapped at her ankles. As they pressed on, the wind had picked up, cutting her bones, algae-stained rocks towering above.

Finally, she crawled onto the open beach. Her legs trembled as the wet sand shifted underfoot, threatening to send her back into the Veil. Her cloak was soaked from hem to hood. Her feet throbbed with each step, raw from the salt and coarse sand that stung her. As she paused, Popelina wondered why such a journey had been necessary. Surely the Oracle knew of this union? If not, why the secrecy? What was there to fear from two distant nations in union? Had recent disputes pushed Tifern and Alkpine apart? If Calliope weren't aware of this wedding, it would explain the secretive nature of this journey. But a secret betrothal? What could the motive be? She considered, anxiety growing within her.

She had been permitted passage through a steerlane on two separate occasions. Once as an infant to attend Calliope's coronation, and then as part of the Imperator's entourage for a trade-treaty. "Perhaps she has not blessed our union?" She worried, that would be controversial, but does my father need to seek blessing from another monarch? There was no precedence for such a thing! But Tifern did control the Veil, and the Veil was power.

Two council guards led the princess across the Reach, not her usual band of servants and attendants. The first, Caladain, she'd known from years, as he'd stood sentry over her skulking through the Citadel's circling stairs and towers. A wide but agile man of medium stature, a cold stare now meeting her enquiring look. Despite earlier assistance over the tumbling rocks, now he merely watched, a cold stare unyielding as she climbed the beach. Did she trust him, fear him even? Something about that stare, troubled her from within. The second guard puzzled her, strong built with tightly curled black hair, roughly tied back to reveal a round face. Who is she? The princess thought as she recovered her breath. The female guard leaned in closer to Caladain, their whispers hurried. Popelina couldn't catch the words, but the occasional glance in her direction set her nerves alight. Something had changed—she was sure of it. What secrets passed between them? Every hurried whisper, feeding at her gnawing suspicion.

After what felt like hours of silent debate, the morning sun had started its climb behind the two soldiers. As it rose, a warming orange glow reflected against the shoreline behind her. Such beauty observing over such chaos, she thought. With the morning arrived, moisture in the air started gain in strength, a far cry from the dry plains of home. Only now, as she stood, did she notice the providence before her. Lush trees of every kind loomed in the distance, spotlights of the morning, effervescently breaking through the towering canopy. The woman lumbered toward her with a clumsy yet determined stride, the weight of heavy hands betraying the raw strength she held.

"Get up. We move. Your new home waits" she said, smug with confidence.

This mysterious voice filled her with unease, but a resilience still stirred within, keeping her wits at the ready. She spoke with a deep grunt, husky with years of smoke abuse – "Not from Alkpine, not Oakston either, nor the South –the Kreiglands perhaps?" It was rumoured there was a people in the open, built strong to live in the flat desert hiding behind the mountain blockade standing between the Oakston basin and the far east coast. Little was known about them, even by the scholars.

This wasn't what she had agreed to.

Straightening her spine, she turned to them both, masking the cauldron of fear bubbling inside.

"Tell me where we are going!" Popelina said.

"You'll know soon enough, child," Caladain replied, now walking toward her. He spoke with a sure, soothing authority, which calmed Popelina out of her building rage.

"Please, I never wanted to marry the forest prince, but I agreed! Something is happening—please, tell me!" Her voice cracking, a plea this time.

"Not Oakston, little girl…" the woman mocked, "you're coming with me, the High-Seer awaits you."

"…not Oakston?" The words struck Popelina like a cold blade, slicing through her resolve like butter. Her breath caught in her throat, heart pounding with disbelief.

The woman's smirk deepened, her hand clawing at Popelina's arm like a vice. "You're mine now, little one," she growled, her voice thick with menace.

"W…Wh…Wha" She stuttered, unable to finish.

"Enough! We must reach Patron before the sun gets too hot, I must take my leave – I am needed south at Barrow." Caladain said, pointing towards a distant bay across the beach, a pointed rock at its centre. Popelina was void as shock drained her expression.

Her mind spiralled, trying to grasp at the truth. What has my father done? How could he… He promised me! She fought hard to understand, but the more she tried, the more her strength drained away, leaving her broken, like a hollow statue of stone.

Too empty to resist, Popelina barely registered the brute lifting her off the ground. Her legs dangled uselessly as they marched South along the coast, the reality settling over her like a weight—her fate was not her own.

The pair carried her for most of the morning, but the steady ache of hunger started to set in. As her senses returned, a pain ached across her side where the plate steel of the brute's armour had dug in.

Struggling for freedom, the woman dropped her harshly onto the sand. Dazed, her mind wandering aimlessly as her eyes focused on the distant horizon. The sharp snap of a wave startled her out of the daze, the sudden cold biting at her fingers as they gripped the sand, pulling her mind back to the present. Caladain appeared beside her to help her as she regained her feet.

"Was that necessary, Narc?" Caladain asked, his voice gentle but firm.

"Eh." The brute grunted, shrugging off the comment.

"Pfft…" He replied, a guiding hand behind the small of her back.

She looked up, the pointed rock rose above her sharply, now a looming presence. It cast a long shadow over her. Expanding far into the sky, the fortress of rough grey stone had been carved from the rock to dominate the scene, a winding staircase just visible across the bay. The forest wall sat behind her, its foreboding presence intensified by the cold weight of the shadow pressing against the midday sun.

As they neared a thin rope bridge, clouds began to fill the sky, humidity rising. Narc nudged her forward onto the narrow rope bridge. At first, the barnacle-encrusted planks felt slippery beneath her, but soon they offered enough grip for her to adjust to the gentle sway from the wind. The bridge must have been three hundred feet long to just two feet wide, guided by two lengths on either side. From here, she could just make out the spray of waves crashing against the jagged rocks of the Reach—a stark reminder of the path she had taken, and the sinking realization that there was no turning back.

Once on the island, the stronghold filled the sky, sheer spikes soaring high, broken only by slanted, bare windows cut into the tower. Two monoliths stood at its base with an intimidating grace, their faded features twisted into a silent warning. The first shaped into a giant worm, rising from the rock, sharp needles protruded from a gaping jaw, its tail continuing past them up the winding stairs.

Forming an arch, the second, stood tall, arm aloft, resting on the worm's side, the other holding a spear like weapon towards the sky. While their features had faded, their overbearing stature warned any who dared to pass. Popelina stared at the fortress in awe. While Alkpine was refined and beautiful, this place was rough, yet grander in scale, oppressively imposing. They passed the arch, climbing in silent pilgrimage along the elongated body of the worm.

After three turns, her feet started to throb, the jagged path poorly maintained. Was the climb meant to weaken those who climbed it? She couldn't help but wonder.

It had taken most of the day, the temperature dropping with each corner as they climbed higher, and higher. Popelina brushed a hand along winding walls to see a story lost to time. Had this creature once roamed the world's oceans? The ancient design of the fortress, and its silence, hinted at a power older than she could fathom. Finally, a great door of chestnut oak stood before them.

The great oak doors groaned open with a thunderous roar, the sound echoing around them as a flood of pure obsidian light poured through the threshold. Blinded by the dark brilliance, Popelina stumbled, her breath caught in her chest. A cool warmth, both chilling and soothing, washed over her, like the tip of a spear coursing through her veins. Her world melted away, the edges of her senses blurring as she stood in awe, pulled deeper by the aura's magnetic embrace.

Then, from within the shimmering light, a figure began to form—slowly, like a shadow stretching into being. At first, a faint silhouette, and then, with terrifying clarity, Vizier Ren.

Popelina blinked, confusion gripping her. He was here, standing before her, calm and composed. She had left him in Alkpine, two days behind.

How could this be?

Chapter Six

Death of a Paladin

Hope walks beside sorrow, a lonely friend –

though its gait is slow, a burdened step may yet find

purpose in the journey.

Godrick, son of Alleric: Notes from the road.

Berwick awoke, muscles stiff from the cramped den he'd carved from the brush, but it was the deeper, raw ache inside that threatened to crush him. His eyes clamped shut with the fear of what he would see, seeing makes it real he managed with resignation.

They are dead, gone. He knew the truth would not hide, he must face it.

Stiff with the cold damp of morning, Berwick forced himself to survey the aftermath of the night, each step heavy with dread.

Bodies, covered in the early dew, lay awakened in the grass– strange faces stared back at him with dull eyes, calling to be laid to rest. He traced the hollow for his brother and father, his heart fluttering. They lay together where they had fallen, bodies entangled in a sea of armour and weaponry, dried blood staining the wet grass. Kneeling beside his father, Berwick placed a trembling hand on his chest. A tear fell down his cheek, he was alone.

Slowly, carefully, he moved them to a more dignified position, laid kindly side by side in peace. He thought of fleeing, but where would he go? Barrow? Had they come from there? He wasn't sure, but seeing his only brother, and friend so still, a quiet determination set within him.

With a weary resolve, Berwick seized an axe cast aside in the struggle and began to dig. Each stroke into the earth guiding the next, as though the ground wanted to open for him. This would be their final home. As Berwick shifted his father, Aleric's sword caught his eye, still shimmering with an iridescent glow. As he shifted his father, a parchment caught his eye, hidden inside the leather jerkin. He pulled it out, frowning at the strange assortment of symbols and characters.

›find my paladin hat fong my step
›bring me his cord
›be wats in patron

They made no sense. He placed it in the satchel across his shoulder and rested a hand on his father's brow.

When a Paladin dies in battle, fighting for his queen, a sacred ritual takes place, with token of gratitude for his service placed in his hands to guide him on his journey. As an outcast, Aleric would receive no such a gift, but Berwick would not leave his father to wander the unknown. He took a small trinket from his bag, whittled into a delicate runic shape from ash, inlaid with precious metal, it was all he had left of his mother, who died when he was born. He placed the ornament gently in Aleric's hands, a final gift for both his father and brother, to mark their sacrifice. Then, with slow, deliberate movements, he pushed the exposed earth over their bodies, as if wrapping them in a blanket, shielding them from the chaos around them. His task complete, he turned to the litter of soldiers. The late morning sun would glint against their armour, as he moved through the hollow – there will be no peace for these eyes he said aloud. He turned to the crest on the breastplate on the nearest soldier – his father's final words echoed in his mind, sharp as the clash of steel—'not the Tifern... Alk...' he had screamed. Alkpine. The circle of the city, pierced by a long spear, marked them as Alkpine soldiers—but how? A regiment of Alkpine soldiers here, in Umidus? How did they cross the Veil? Suspicion furrowing his brow. He took the note from his satchel once more, seeing the broken wax revealing seal of the Vizier – I must find the meaning of this text, I will follow this thread.

Only when the last flicker of light vanished from their empty eyes did Berwick turn away, leaving the ashes to the wind and the land, alone in his purpose.

With a single cause now driving him, Berwick prepared for the road ahead. He filled his satchel with the meagre supplies they carried—rye bread, dried berries, and jerky, wrapped in linen. A sturdy branch served as his staff, supporting his weary legs, while his father's sword lay hidden beneath the grey cloak draped over his shoulders.

He set his course north, though his destination remained unclear. Perhaps Oakston, he thought. The forest folk were known for their kindness to strangers, and perhaps they could help him decipher the mysterious note his father had left behind.

The journey would take a week by foot, crossing vast stretches of vibrant grassland—teeming with life by day, yet cloaked in fog by night. But Berwick knew the Steppe well, its rhythm of life had been the backdrop to his nomadic years. Berwick set into a steady rhythm, alternating between brisk strides and long leaps, covering much ground under the broad sky.

After two days trekking, he paused at a clear stream, nibbling at the last of the meat jerky he had brought. He watched the water cascaded over rock, fish fighting against the current as they hunted a tasty morsel on the surface.

A twig snapped, followed by a rustle, and then— out of the brush—a heavy mass of a man barrelled into Berwick, knocking him off his feet.

Caught unawares, Berwick tumbled back into the stream as a haughty laugh bellowed from the figure. Berwick scrambled to his feet, brushing the dust from his breeches, his soaked rear a remnant of the fall. As he eyed the man before him, the danger seemed to ebb. Surveying his opponent, he sensed the danger had passed. The man stood a full foot shorter than Berwick, but his broad arms and thick, tree-trunk legs showed great strength beyond his height. He wore dark green, blending him into the background, yet a fine gold trim betrayed some form of nobility. A long, dark beard, tied at his chin, set his blue sharp eyes, beneath a heavy brow that glared with suspicion. His gaze fell to Berwick's sword, poking through his ruffled cloak.

"What's that, boy? A sky-blade, is it? Think you'll be using that on me, eh?' the man barked, his eyes narrowing with suspicion.

"N-nothing! Who are you?' Berwick stammered, his voice edged with uncertainty.

"N'er you mind that – who are you, poking around my land?" He snapped.

"B-Berwick, but you can call me Wick. I'm heading to the forest basin for help from the treefolk."

"Aid, eh? What's wrong with ya then? Ahh, just as well—wouldn't want to scuff up that pretty head of yours, eh?" the man replied. His bulky arms falling to his side, relaxing his posture. He paused.

"Ok, ok, sorry for the alarm. Names Taronuicus, Taro if you will. Yes, yes I am of the forest, a little away from home mind. What this talk of aid here ay?" He continued.

"My father, brother was murdered, Alkpine soldiers, I need help!" he pleaded, the panic was audible in his voice, trembling as he spoke the words.

"Don't be daft, that dozy lot can't swim!"

"Here, I have proof" Berwick handed Taro the parchment, the forester twirling it in his hands, rubbing the red wax seal with intrigue.

"Hmm…" Was all he managed.

"Funny thing, I'm after that lot too. Promised me a bride, they did. The snake Ren thinks he can play me for a fool! Says he wants an alliance, fat chance of that now eh! I thought perhaps I might travel over the Steer at the Oracles pleasure, she does love to see 'em squirm" he rambled, deeper now, relaxed, and rhotic.

Taro paused, softening as he took in Berwick's slumped shoulders and defeated stance.

"Listen eh, Wick? I'll take you back to my people, we have one who might translate this nonsense for ya – then if needs be, we will stain that round city with the shit on my shoe eh? Sound good?" A kindness took over the tension in Taro's eyes, Berwick saw something there that he trusted, fuelling him with hope.

The pair continued their journey together, swapping stories and sharing merriment. A morning's walk from the forest border, the dwarfed man sat by the fire, grabbing a bowl of wild carrots and rodent stew from the boy. With a satisfied sigh, he settled onto a stump.

"There's a song for a night like this, Wick. Clear moonlit sky, no breeze—we call it Miya's Light," Taro said, pulling a wooden flute from his pack.

When Miya walks and lights the sky,

Her golden glow falls soft and slow.

Minor trails her close behind,

In silver's shade, their hearts aglow.

A pair that never part,

Through darkest nights and shifting tides,

One by the other, every night,

Their strength always abides.

When the path is hard to see,

And winds blow gentle too,

Look to the sky, to find the light,

That stays forever true.

So walk beside me, steady hand,

As Miya walks this quiet land.

Through light and dark, we'll find our way,

For strength in two will never sway.

Taro fell silent, turning his gaze to the nurturing crackle of the fire. In the distance, crickets sang softly in harmony with his tune, as Berwick drifted into a slumber beneath Miya's protective glow. "I've lived in this world for long enough to know it's fragility Wick, I've spent years in my brother's shadow much like yourself there, and worked hard to find my place by 'is side. We fight in an eternal struggle for what we believe in, but honestly, I just want peace, a warm fire, an honest woman, and strong mead. A place where the leaders of the world are chosen on merit and not inheritance." The words sat heavy on Taro, a burden he carried. "If that world doesn't exist friend, lets make it" Wick replied, a hand on his shoulder.

Chapter Seven

A Silent Council

Only the blind strike with anger, for when the wind changes, the blade catches only air. But listen to the wind, and strike with your enemy's doubt.

Qadi, Scrollmaster to Lysander: The Veil's Whisper

The Vizier's Hall was a place of governance, yet grandeur still clung to it in the delicate details. A long, imposing table stretched the length of the room, worn smooth by years of polite debate. Shafts of pale sunlight pierced through the narrow, arched windows set high along the stone walls, casting lines of brilliance across the polished walnut surface. Columns flanked each side, hosting guards that stood unnervingly still, as their shadows swallowed the light. The golden seal of Alkpine, a circle pierced by a long spear, was carved into the centre of the table, and emblazoned on the backs of each councillor's chair, as a reminder of the weight of their duty. The same seal decorated their robes, stitched in rich thread, and hung in faded splendour on a vast tapestry at the far end of the room.

Towering over them all, set slightly above the table on a raised dais, sat Lysander. It was a seat normally left empty, a symbolic gesture of power that belonged to the council in this chamber. But today, Lysander sat heavily upon it, his figure looming. His posture was stiff with anger, his face flush, a red hue creeping up his neck, and his hand clenched tightly around the arm of the throne, knuckles white as his fury brewed.

"Ren-." His voice bellowed through the hall.

"That worm, he deceived us!" His hand slamming against the armrest, cracking the wooden frame. The sound echoed through the chamber, yet the council sat still, unmoving, their faces unreadable, eyes downcast.

"Patron, my spies tell me – Patron! That old relic of ruin!" Lysander continued, standing now, his eyes wild with the fire of his indignation. "You think I am blind to his schemes? He undermines me—undermines all of us! And what do you do? Nothing!" His voice rose to a, filling the space, his frustration now all-consuming. He gestured wildly, his fingers trembling as they cut through the air.

The council remained unmoved, their silence a wall against his fury. Scrollmaster Hoplite, a man hunched with age, shuffled in his seat, daring to lift his head. His voice, when it came, was barely a whisper, "Your grace... what would you have us do?"

Lysander turned on him, eyes blazing. "What would I have you do?" His laugh was bitter. "I would have you act! I would have you—" He slammed his fist down again, this time splitting the wood beneath him. "Raise an army! Burn Patron to the ground if we must!"

A silence fell over the room, colder now, dangerous. Varang, the Armsmaster, raised an eyebrow but said nothing. Coinmaster Ryo leaned forward slightly, adjusting the silver trim of his robe as if to steady himself. "Your grace," Ryo ventured cautiously, "the cost of such an endeavour—crossing the Veil—requires permission from Tifern. It would be..."

"Costly?" Lysander spat the word. "The cost is nothing compared to the ruin we will face if we allow my daughter to remain captive! And what of the Oakston prince, he is expecting a bride!"

Ryo opened his mouth to respond, but a glare from Lysander silenced him. The Imperator's hand slammed down once more, this time with a finality that made the air in the room seem to still. "Summon the ambassador of Tifern. We will cross the Veil. And Patron will burn." His voice was cold now, the fire of his earlier rage tempered into something far more dangerous.

The weight of the Imperator's decision hanging heavy over them, the seal of Alkpine glinting in the shafts of sunlight as if bearing silent witness to the act that would follow.

"No longer, will I suffer this. For too long have I let the string be pulled, limiting my resolve – but no more, no more." He finished, almost in a whisper.

Chapter Eight

Echoes of the Past

"When history is written in the moment, the truth is marred by the passing of time. But, when history is critiqued by its ancestors, the true becomes the moment."

The Oracle: The Book of Lore.

Ren stepped out of the twisting darkness into his old chambers, the faint hum of its energy dissipating as the air settled around him. The exertion was growing with each journey through the void, he took a moment to take in his surroundings. The room was undisturbed from his hasty departure six weeks prior. The cold stone walls were lined with leather-bound books and rolls of parchment. A well-used horseshoe desk stood at the centre bearing the dried ink stains from his final writings. The room had its familiar smell of dust and papers, stacks of the latter strewn across the chamber.

"Ren?"

A voice startled him, though he masked his surprise. At the far end of the room, near a towering shelf of strange and contorted specimens, stood Qadi, Scrollmaster to Lysander. The man's robes were plain yet immaculate, a rich crimson and silver velvet. His hands were clasped behind his back in a posture of both curiosity and caution.

"Ah, yes. Qadi." Ren replied smoothly, stepping fully into the room. His far darker robes, rustled softly as he moved. "Still lurking among the scrolls, I see. Some things never change."

"And yet, some things do," Qadi said, his eyes narrowing as they swept over Ren's attire. "Those are new, I assume. Certainly not of the Imperator's tailors."

Ren allowed himself a faint smile. "Observant as always. The past rarely clings to me for long."

Qadi tilted his head, studying Ren as one might a strange artifact. "So it seems. Though your timing is curious. The Imperator's wrath still lingers in this chamber. I doubt you've come to placate him."

Ren's smile tightened. "Lysander moves to anger to hastily, his mind burns as fiery as ever. But his rage is misdirected. He wishes you to march on Patron, does he not?"

Qadi's jaw tightened, but he gave a small nod. "Through the Reach. There is no other path."

"It will fail," Ren said flatly, his gaze drifting toward the room's lone window. Outside, the night was dark and unyielding, the stars hidden behind thick clouds. "But it must happen."

Qadi frowned, stepping closer. "You speak as though you've already seen it?"

Ren turned back to face him, his expression inscrutable. "Let us say that my perspective has been expanded. There are forces at play that Lysander cannot hope to grasp. The march will humble him—temper him even. It is necessary for what is to come."

"You speak in riddles, Ren," Qadi said sharply. "Necessary for whom? Yourself? This... higher power? I'm not blind. That mark, the Veilstorm—it's no mortal sigil."

Ren stepped forward, his voice dropping to a calm, measured tone. "And it is that insight, that curiosity, which makes you valuable to me, Qadi. I have not come to threaten you or to make you my enemy. I have come to ask for your help."

Qadi stiffened, though his expression betrayed the faintest flicker of intrigue. "My help?"

"Of everyone on this council, only you will see to reason," Ren said, gesturing to the scrolls lining the walls. "Your knowledge of the world and its history is second only to the records we keep in Patron. You see patterns where others see chaos. That is why I trusted you once, and why I trust you still. Lysander's path is his own, but you must prepare him for what lies beyond this march. There will be moments... decisions... that only you will see clearly enough to guide."

Qadi's brow furrowed, his hands tightening behind his back. "And what am I to prepare him for, exactly? Speak plainly, Ren."

"I cannot," Ren said simply. "Not yet."

"Then what can you offer me?"

Ren's gaze softened, and for a moment, the weight of his new purpose grew heavy on his shoulders. "Reassurance. You are in no danger from me, old friend I live now for something greater," Ren said, his tone low but certain. "Far beyond the Imperium. Its purpose is not to destroy but to reshape—to prepare for what is to come."

Qadi's lips thinned, pausing to reflect on his former master's words. "I will do as you ask but know this. If you move against Alkpine, I will not receive you again. My allegiance will always be to Alkpine, to the Council, and to the Imperium. I will not betray Lysander, Ren, no matter how fond I am of you. Be sure of this path you traverse before it consumes you."

Ren nodded, his expression calm. "I would expect no less and will heed your warning old friend. But if you truly serve Alkpine, then take note: observe, record, and prepare for what is to come. The path ahead is darker than even you can imagine."

A tense silence hung between them, broken only by the faint whistle of wind against the stone walls. Qadi's expression softened, and he gave a reluctant nod.

"I will keep your secrets," he said, his voice low. "For now. But do not test my loyalty, Ren. Whatever power you serve, remember this, we are not your pawns."

Ren inclined his head, his smile faint but genuine. "A fair warning. And one I shall hear. Now, I must leave, you have a visitor..."

Qadi stepped aside as Ren pulled a chain out from the inside of his robes. Taenite curled around a brilliant green gem that shone in the light. He thought a moment of Lysander, his former master, a tinge of regret crossing his mind. A fleeting image, Ren turned the stone in his hand, and the air around him shimmered like heat over a stove. A low hum reverberated through the chamber, building to a deafening tone that sent parchment fluttering from the desk. In an instant, the light engulfed him, and he was gone, leaving only a faint metallic smell in his wake.

A light knock rapped at the door, pulling Qadi from his thoughts. He glanced at the faint shimmer left behind by the portal, its energy fading but the weight of Ren's words still pressing heavily on his mind.

"Yes," Qadi said, his voice steadier than he felt.

A young messenger stepped inside, his face pale, his eyes darting nervously around the room. "Varang, my lord," he said cautiously. "He wishes to discuss strategy."

Qadi nodded curtly, brushing dust from his robes as if shedding the remnants of Ren's presence. "I will go to him. Give me a moment."

The messenger bowed and retreated, leaving Qadi alone once more. For a moment, he let his gaze linger on the scrolls lining the walls, his fingers twitching with the urge to record what had just transpired. But not yet. Not now.

Turning toward the door, he straightened his posture and exhaled slowly, forcing his thoughts into order. Whatever path lay ahead, it would be his duty to prepare.

***

It had almost been a year since his summoning. It started on a lonely evening towards the end of Vernal, the season of renewal, where Ren looked out from his keep towards the Veil. As deepnight settled the sky, Minor hid passively behind her sister. He watched the moons passing, deep in thoughts, when a deep cast of emerald radiance blinded his view. That night, and every night since, Ren's dreams became plagued with visions. He saw many things, from crashing waves to the Veilstorm itself lording over Oracle in its depths. Noone alive had ever witnessed the beast, yet what he saw matched the horror described in the earliest texts with explicable detail. Yet it couldn't be true, he saw a horror of gigantic proportions erupting from the Veil, a thousand folds of dark leathery skin forming into a great serpent. He would push the thought deep into his conscious, fearful of what it could mean.

He also saw a place beyond the Veil, to the north of Umidus where a shard of rock was waiting. Winding stairs beckoning him forward. After many sleepless nights, he finally surrendered to the pull.

After the climb, Patron appeared before him, a ruin of ancient halls long abandoned, yet a strange energy was captured within stone. As he wandered the fortress, the dreams that had haunted him sharpened into reality. He silently crept into a wide chamber, where they were waiting.

An alter sat in the centre, symbols edged into the rock.

⋂♀⛓⋂

"Chosen" voiced whispered.

Their voices echoed, not spoken but pressed into his mind like the tolling of a great bell. The chamber was lit by an unnatural glow emanating from the braziers that marked the walls. The Guardians cloaked their signature black robes stood to welcome him to their agency. It was here that he first heard of the Oracle's final prophecy, not one of destruction, but of providence. It too was etched into the stone alter.

᛫WEN FAL ƧAL TƆr ƟrAKL ƧLƐP
᛫UNTIL ΓALƧ ΓAL WATEr WƐP

"When the Veil shall tear, the Oracle will sleep.

Until the false are fallen, and the waters weep."

The haunting rhyme followed him. It was burned into his mind, like the marking of cattle with heated steel.

Since that day, the Guardians shared their knowledge with Ren anointing him in their mission, to enable the true Oracle's return. They had given him the chain, its brilliant green stone shimmering with its radiant hue of green. Yet, he was warned, each use of its power would exact a toll on his mortal body.

Ren stepped out of the portal into the heart his new home, the ancient fortress was carved into the island, raising high into the clouds. The cool air clung to his robes as he steadied himself against the sharp bite of exhaustion, the cost of crossing through ever higher. Above, the spire-like cliffs towered over him, their jagged edges stretching toward the sky, cutting through the dense fog that veiled the bay.

Waiting for his return was the statuesque Guardian Throth. He was heavily aged and veiled in an air of mystery. His gaze—fixed on him as he approached.

"You return," Throth's voice reverberated in Ren's mind, low and weighty.

Ren offered a small incline of his head. "I need a moment. To reflect."

Throth shifted slightly, as though considering the request, before fading back into the mist without a word. Ren exhaled, the weight of his presence lifting as he turned towards a narrow pathway.

Now standing in Patron's shadow once more, Ren felt the weight of their words pressing down on him. The betrayal of Lysander had been necessary, he reminded himself. The Imperator was shackled to the powers of the false one, and Ren saw something greater ahead, a purpose that transcended the petty conflicts of the Imperium.

The faces of those he had left behind haunted him—the loyalty he had forsaken, the trust he had broken. His fingers tightened around the chain beneath his robes, its cold metal a reminder of the power he now wielded and the price he had would pay.

He glanced back towards the door. Throth waited just beyond, but for now, he allowed himself a moment to stand in the silence of the fortress, the echoes of his past and the weight of his future colliding.

Chapter Nine

The Winding Road Begins

Does time flow like a river, unhurried and sure?

Or like a torrent carving through a crumbling landscape?

Perhaps both—does balance not guide this world?

Median, King of Trees: Words in the Wood

The forest absorbed every sound as they moved, Berwick trailing close behind Taro as they stepped onto a cobbled path that followed a fast-moving river.

High above, figures glided silently across raised platforms, their bows slack but vigilant. Berwick felt the weight of their eyes, a reminder that not everyone who entered was welcomed.

As they climbed, the oaks thinned into tall pines, their trunks stretching toward the sky. The crisp air stung Berwick's lungs, while Taro pressed on with ease. Children ran along the riverbank, their laughter drifting through the trees. "You're slowing, Wick," Taro called back with a chuckle.

Berwick pressed forward, his legs straining as the path climbed steadily alongside the river. At a ridge, the trees parted to reveal the city, woven into the forest itself. Rope bridges crisscrossed between the platforms high in the canopy, and the moss-covered longhouses, which clung to the cliffs. Below, the river wound through the city.

"There she is," Taro said, pride swelling in his voice. Oakston's Heart. Not like them stone cities, eh?." Berwick stood frozen, overwhelmed by the sight.

"Our people have lived here since before the Veil broke. The trees and mountains keep us safe. Always have, always will."

As they descended into the city, Berwick noticed the people around him. Like Taro, they were shorter, standing a full head beneath Berwick, yet could be seen carrying water and forage twice their size. They wore furs stitched with hide to provided layers of warmth and protection against the cold mist that settled within the trees.

At last, Taro paused before a grand building, its roof heavy with moss and brambles, draped in fresh blackcurrants. The earthy scent of the forest mingling with the damp air. Taro led the way with a confident stride, pushing open the wide, carved doors at its head. Berwick followed close behind, eyes adjusting to the dim firelight within.

The longhouse stretched far deeper than Berwick had expected, its dark-honey beams vanishing into the smoky shadows of tobacco and herbs. Woodsmoke and pine fought in the air, drifting from the warmth of the hearth."

Flickering lanterns cast dancing shadows along the length of the hall, illuminating carvings of twisted trees and prancing animals etched deep into the wood.

Rows of heavy benches lined a pit of glowing embers, which dominated the middle of the room, its heat rising to meet the chilly air as it crept in from the forest. The far end of the hall was dominated by a raised chair, carved from the gnarled root of an ancient willow, its twisted roots and branches reaching from floor to ceiling.

Berwick's eyes lingered on the soft pelts and intricate weavings that covered the courtiers who filled the benches. There was wealth here, woven subtly into the fabric of the room—a glint of gems catching the firelight as sweet honey wine and scraps covering the tables. As the pair approached the throne, their conversation hushed, eyes fixed on the newcomer with curiosity.

Taro gestured toward the raised throne a few feet away "That's my father," he whispered, "we won't bother him much, it's Lohith, my elder brother, we need to speak with." He finished as they approached the chair.

"Father," Taro greeted with a slight bow. "I've returned with news,"

"And with guest," The old man enquired, his voice was soft and slow but carried still carried a weight of authority.

"A welcome sight my son. And you, young traveller. Sit. Share in our bread and meat."

Servants moved quickly, setting platters before them. The food was simple but hearty—warm bread and roasted meat, a welcome feast for tired feet.

In a distant corner, Lohith, arms folded, watched the gathering. His frame, like Taro's, was stout, but with more a more a refined presence and thoughtful features. His tunic, more ornate that those around him, was lined with grey wolf fur, adorned in leather and charms, his dark, braided hair tied back, and jaw, fixed and square.

As Berwick ate, his gaze drifted to Lohith, their eyes locking for a moment. Something in that stare unsettled him, a dart of tension tightening in his gut "Come," Taro said. "It's time we spoke to my brother."

They approached Lohith, he nodded towards a passage, leading them through the hidden archway. His eyes fixed, he turned to assess the stranger with a quick intensity.

It was a small office, the chatter of the great hall falling into the background. Berwick lowered his head to fit through the doorway. Two stools sat at a low table in the centre, a map of the forest pinned down against it by a haughty serrated blade. Light from the hearth flickered through the narrow doorway, casting suspense into the room.

"Taronuicus," Lohith's voice was low, careful. His eyes flicked to his brother. "And this?"

"A friend," Taro replied. "We bring news brother, troubling news."

Lohith was shorter than Taro yet commanded the room they entered.

"Tell me, what is it brother, did you find the Alkpine girl?"

Berwick handed over the note. Lohith's forehead knotted as he scanned the message, each symbol etching concern into his features.

"This…" Lohith muttered, rubbing a hand across his chin. "This does changes things,"

Taro stepped forward with anticipation, his face darkened, as Berwick stayed back. Lohith continued, "It is an old text, Annulumic. Strange times indeed.

"Find the Paladin that roams the Steppe, bring me his sword. She waits in Patron."

"She… the princess?" Taro responded, aghast.

"Likely, but I cannot say."

Turning to Berwick, "Your father was this Paladin I take it? Got mixed up in a dark scheme by the looks of it – what is his fate?" Lohith said.

"H-he died, we were attacked, near Barrow" Berwick's voice stumbled as the battle flashed across his mind, he shifted, exposing his father's sword, which flashed in the dull light.

"Ahh. His sword—it was your his, yes?" Lohith said, his eyes narrowing as he pointed toward the gleaming blade.

"It was, I suppose it is mine now." Berwick resigned.

"I met your father, Alleric? Many moonrises ago I travelled to see the new Oracle, the King wished to pay homage or some nonsense. That sword, and the man who carried it – you never forget such a thing."

Unsure how to respond, Berwick stayed silent, staring at the parchment in Lohith's thick fingers. He folded it carefully before handing it back to Berwick. "I understand your concern, brother," he said to Taro, his voice steady, "but we cannot act rashly. This will need a delicate hand."

"Brother, they insult us—this house, this forest. We cannot let it go unanswered," Taro insisted, his voice rising.

"It won't," Lohith replied, his tone calm but unyielding. "But if the princess is captive in Patron, the Imperator does not yet know. We must move with care. This requires precision, not fury—but you have my support."

"Then what must we do, brother?"

"Go to Patron, Taro, but quietly. Seek the princess, if indeed she is still held there, learn what you can. We must know the truth behind these schemes."

"It's rough terrain past the forest, Lohith." Taro asked.

"We cannot risk a war. We don't know who or what we're fighting against. Dark times, indeed—you must travel light and fast." He paused, eyes narrowing. "Take the boy and return when you know more."

"Very well, brother—I hope you are right," Taro finished, his voice heavy with doubt.

Chapter Ten

Captive

A path diverges. One leads to the edge, the other,

a fall. Both are shrouded, hiding the dawn of fate.

Guardian Throth, The Book of Lore, Vol. II

Poppy's breath was steady, but her mind was lost in distain. The room around her glowed faintly as a soft light crept from the square lamps built into the walls. The air was cool, flowing gently from the bare windows, naked to the night. She sat upright at a desk, staring out into distance, a reflection of the day she left her home. This room, however, was stark, the niceties of her former life a distant memory. Nonetheless, she was comfortable, a quilted bed of down feather was set into the wall behind her, while an array of purple silks draped over an intricate privy dressing. Symbols were hidden throughout the room's design, yet they were unfamiliar to the young princess.

On the farthest wall, a heavy oak door, stood between her and her freedom. Fixed to the dark wood, a sigil had captured her view. In its centre, a spiked, curling shape, stood out, reminiscent of the toothed worm at the Patron's Gate. The crest was surrounded by a field of spears that appeared to ripple, as though gliding through the air. Beneath the serpent, more symbols of unknown meaning.

'GArdIOO OF hU FAL.

She rose from her chair, pacing lightly across the stone floor, her steps echoing lightly. *What is this place? What has the Vizier become?* Thoughts spiralled through her mind. She had known him her whole life, a trusted advisor to her father—now a stranger, hiding behind the face she used to know.

A soft rap at the door interrupted her thoughts. The door clicked open without waiting for her response. Ren stepped across the threshold. He was flanked by Caladain, who locked the door behind them.

Both wore velvet purple robes, simple in design. The same crest that had adored the door was embroidered prominently over their chests. The sight of it on Ren's clothing made her stomach twist. *Who is he, truly?*

"Comfortable, I hope?" Ren's voice was smooth, contemplative. He moved with a careful elegance, his hands clasped behind his back as he glided into the room. An air of satisfaction hung about him.

Poppy stiffened, her fists curling at her sides. "Comfortable?" she echoed, her voice low with contempt. "You bring me here, under false pretences, across fierce storms and battering waves, lock me away in an old crumbling tower, and you ask if I am comfortable?"

Ren smirked, but said nothing at first, letting the silence stretch uncomfortably between them. He took a few steps closer, his eyes sweeping over the room before landing on her.

"This place is not a prison, Popelina. It's a sanctuary," Ren said, his voice calm but tinged with a grating arrogance. "You're safe here."

She scoffed. "Safe from what? My father?"

"Your father knew nothing of this," Ren cut her off, his words sharp, cutting. Popelina felt a twinge of fear. "The Imperator has been… kept abreast of our plans but knows nothing of our true intentions. The work we do here is of great importance."

Popelina stepped forward, her defiance flaring. "Great importance! He is your King! You play dark games here, Vizier. Do you dare to conspire against my father? You think you can control me is that it?"

Ren's smile faded, his gaze hardening. "Control you?" He stepped closer, his presence looming over her. "I have no need to control you, Popelina of Aridus. You are exactly who you need to be."

Her heart raced, anger pulsing through her veins, but she forced herself to keep her composure. "Who I need to be? And who is that?" she asked, her voice full of resentment.

Ren's eyes flicked briefly to the crest upon the door, and for a moment, there was a shadow hesitation, "There are things that you do not yet understand my dear princess. A power far older, far deeper th—"

She cut him off, her voice rising. "Enough riddles, Vizier! Tell me why I am here!"

For a moment, there was silence. Ren's eyes met hers, unblinking. Then he took a step back towards Caladain, stood vigil. He exhaled slowly, the cold composure returning. "You will know dear child, when the time is right, when you are ready."

Her frustration boiled over. In a flash, she darted to the desk, a sharp quill lay atop a piece of blank parchment. She grabbed it, spinning back to face Ren, moving in a blur as she slashed wildly at his forearm.

The quill pierced his skin, drawing a thin line of blood.

Ren looked down at the scratch, his lips twitching, with mild amusement. "Yes," he murmured, "theirs is a fire in you princess. Good." His eyes lingered on her trembling hand, the quill still poised. 'You'll need that fire, soon enough."

She stood, panting, her hand released the quill still in her grip, eyes wide with fear.

Ren tilted his head slightly, studying her reaction, and turned to leave, motioning to Caladain. "We will talk again," he said, his voice smooth as silk. "When you've calmed down."

As he stepped through the doorway, Popelina felt her legs weaken, her defiance ebbing. Caladain's eyes lingered on her for a moment longer, his face unreadable. He locked the door behind them as a note fluttered to the floor.

Popelina took the note and sank onto the bed, her mind racing, questions running through her mind.

Her eyes flicked back to the crest on the reverse, its winding scales a shimmering circle. Whatever Ren held her for, she knew one thing—she had to escape. And soon.

Chapter Eleven

A Rescue

The lion, lonely yet powerful, dominates the plains. But strike him through the heart, and he will writhe with empty purpose. The fox, however, cunning, and deceptive, strikes not with strength, but with stealth and guile.

Qadi, Scrollmaster to Lysander: The Veil's Whisper

Lysander sat rigid on the back of his stallion, a glowing white beast, decorated with plumage and pomp. The heat of the late afternoon sun beat down on the city. The Cenotaph loomed above him, its dolomite arches—like the Citadel itself—catching the light as a towering testament to Alkpine's resilience. Below him, the square was filled with onlookers, their faces hidden behind the unbroken lines of guards, lances aloft. The steel shimmered, holding the crowd at a safe distance.

The Cenotaph place the heart of the city, seat of the council's power. Behind him, Varang, Hoplite, Ryo, and Qadi stood in a neat line, heads bowed, like children scorned. A choir of conspiracy muttering under their breath. As the façade towered, their eyes cast down with calculating ambition.

Ahead, under the shade of the tower, five soldiers stood at attention, their black armour ringing the sunlight. "You will henceforth be named the Elite Guard" the Imperator cried, his voice carried through the winding web of streets. Dress-spears, as rigid and unyielding as their stance, stood proudly above their heads. Lysander's horse stirred, stirrups waving in the breeze—the earthy air plagued with muck and dust.

Lysander steadied on his horse, sweeping over the crowd. His heart thundered, anger sat in his chest. The betrayal of Ren weighed heavily upon him, but he could not show weakness. Not here. Not now, this was his defining moment.

The Steer's ships blockaded the harbour, visible just outside of the sea wall, preventing all passage across the Veil. In the middle-distance, the Great Torch cradled its blackened lamp, marking the border of the siege.

Lysander inhaled deeply, listing to the crashing waves in their protest– the only sound audible in the silent square. His hand rested on the hilt of his sword as he began.

"People of Alkpine!" His voice boomed across the city, silencing even the sea. "We stand on the precipice of history. Forces move against us, forces that seek to undermine the foundation of this great city!"

The sun's heat pressed down on his back, yet Lysander sat tall, his figure framed by the grandeur of the Cenotaph. His horse shifted once more, a reflection of the restlessness he contained within.

"Ren—Vizier to this great council, who sat beside me in governance—has betrayed us!" The crowd stirred, shock rippling. "But know this" silencing the faces that stared back "—Alkpine will not cower before his treachery!

Nor will we bend to the false Oracle, whose power strangles our trade!"

His soldiers were firm, unblinking, their eyes locked ahead, plumes of black wavering in the air.

"For too long, we have tolerated her control of the Veil, kept in chains of dependency. But no more. Today, we rise against this them, against the lies whispered in the dark!"

"We stand for Alkpine! For our future! And today, these brave soldiers will march to meet this challenge head-on. On two fronts, we will win victory against animosity. The five before you will cross the Reach, destroying Ren and his conspirators, to send fear into Tifern's heart. Our armies will cross the Veil unharmed to take what is rightfully ours!"

His soldiers' armour, polished and bright, gleamed with purpose. Lysander's gaze drifted to them, his voice growing quieter, more deliberate. "You fight not just for this city, but for your children, for the generations that will follow. You must not fall."

As his voice echoed a ripple of approval spread through the crowd.

Lysander raised his hand, his voice once more valiant. "Go now and may the light of Miya and Minor guide you. Bring back my daughter!"

Turning in trained perfection, they marched through the crowd, their footsteps ringing heavy on the cobblestones. The crowd watched in awe, a path parting as they moved toward Muddy Gate. Lysander remained seated upon his horse, his gaze lingering on them as they disappeared from his view.

For a long moment, an awkward silence grew.

A solitary figure caught Lysander's eye. Standing in the shadow, a cloaked figure watched closely over the proceedings. A hood obscuring their face, but Lysander's instincts flared as the figure's cloak shifted, it was a Paladin.

In the same movement, the figure vanishing. Lysander's jaw tightened. A spy, no doubt, sent by Calliope he thought. The Oracle's agents were watching.

Chapter Twelve

The Cunning Desert Fox

As the horned viper coils in wait, the mouse walks free, unaware of the impending danger. But the mouse hides a secret, and both may perish.

Calliope, Oracle: New Lore

A burnt dusk clung to the horizon, streaks of purple and red stretching across the arid sky. Haru watched as a storm circled in the distance, sending sand whirling through the air. Cut deep into the side of a mountain refuge, his chambers felt like an oasis of calm indulgence against the desert's harsh backdrop. Inside, the room was carved with a delicate hand, to provide space for a large round bed, and writing desk against the wall, where bunches of desert thyme and bay hung from protrusions in the wall. The surface was cool to touch, refreshing against the warm heat that ebbed from the dunes.

    The air was thick with the fragrance of saffron and cinnamon, mingling with the soothing notes of lavender and bergamot that drifted from a hammered copper bath at the room's centre. Steam rose from the surface, a layer of sweet oils disturbed by the opulent body reflected in the water.

A need for power flickered over Ayame's mind as she reclined, her skin glowing softly in the amber light, a strand of beads clicking faintly at her breast as she shifted. A seductive gaze sent tingling shivers through the prince, he could not deny his desire for her, she played it well.

Haru floated towards the bed, his midnight-blue robes trailing gently in his wake. His eyes reflected the light of a brazier, flickering softly above the doorway with anticipation. She was dangerous, he knew it, but could not resist her pull.

The bed was draped in linin and damask, delicately embroidered with patterns of the swirling desert winds. He pushed aside the curtain, placing his robe and belt on the oche sheet. An elegant, curved taenite blade, polished to iridescence was laid on top of a burgundy tussled throw.

Ayame's voice broke the silence as she lifted her eyes toward him, arms raising out of the water with a sensual waft of sweet oils. "The moons are aligning, Haru. Ren is in our pocket, and Tifern set to fall. You see it, don't you?"

Haru's gaze drifted from the bed to his lover. As she rose, her dark olive skin shimmered, droplets of water clinging to her curves. He stood still, his face captivated by her body. "I see it," he said, his voice whispered. "...b-but Ren is not a fool. He moves in ways we cannot predict."

The water rippled as she stepped out, the smell of lavender was encapsulating. " Portals, this girl? No, Haru, we hold the Oracle's secret – and when that truth is revealed, Tifern will crumble...."

His expression hardened, should he stop this, could he? "So you do not believe in his tales of the Veilstorm, of the true Oracle? The teeth alone—"

Moving closer, her fingers traced the length of his arm as she leaned in, her lips brushing his ear. He knew her game—her touch against his will, Haru's resistance faltered, just as she had known it would. "Maybe. But you my love, you and I, we will shape the chaos they leave behind."

"So, my love – what next?" he said, breathless.

Ayame's thick lips curled into a seductive smile as she pressed against him, her body gleaming in the low light.

"Her emissary awaits your audience," Ayame reminded him, her tone soft, almost coaxing. "Delay for now. Leave him to ponder his offer some more." She held him now firmly with promise, her wet hair clinging to his shoulders as she placed a hand on his chest. Haru intoxicated, traced her neck, his touch lingering, until

Ayame's lips caressed his, it was all consuming. As she led him to the bed, her eyes caught the mountains beyond. A fleeting thought passed through her mind, "this is only the beginning, I will be queen."

Chapter Thirteen

Letter to Ren from Haru

It is with unwavering resolve that I write you these words, knowing full well the consequences they bring. From our first council, I doubted your vision—a world reshaped by the power of the Veil, free from the corruption of those who seek dominion over it, and I now see that your path you walk is not one of liberation but of chaos.

You promised alliance, yet your actions sow destruction. Rumours from the north have reached me of an army of zealots, who you plan to march against Umidus. As such, I will no longer serve as a pawn in your schemes. My sword lies only with Heurnanon, and its sea of sands.

Know this, Heurn will not fall prey to this hoard. Should you march against me or the Oracle's lands, you will find no ally in the dunes. You will face a desert that swallows its enemy's whole.

This is not a declaration of war, but a warning. You have chosen your path; I have chosen mine. Pray they do not cross.

Haru, Prince of Dunes

Chapter Fourteen

Unwanted Council

Through patience and skill, we may read the signs that the tides write. The storm that breaks is never the storm we expect.

The Oracle: The Book of Lore

The skies above Tifern were an endless expanse of blue, Dampfall had yet to reach the city below which flourished in its radiance. Palm trees lined the streets, their lush fronds swaying gently in the warm breeze. White stone buildings, polished smooth, gleamed under a golden sun. Domes of verdant copper crowned the skyline, their surfaces glowing like jewels against the sky. Vibrant stalls filled the central plaza with the smell of spiced meats, fresh fruits, and flowers. A paradise of abundance, the people walked with ease in flowing togas, unburdened by the troubles of the world beyond.

The High Gardens stood apart from the thriving city, a marble sanctuary of prayer and reflection. Perched atop the cliffs, gardens afforded an unparalleled view of the Veil below, its stirring waters a foreboding reminder of the storm that once tore the land asunder. Its interior was no less impressive, with beams of light streaming through the arches and columns. The air was perfumed with the jasmine and orange blossom, flush with the sound of flowing water and fountain spray.

Standing at a terrace in quiet solitude, Calliope watched as a ship bound for Aridus raised its sails, tightening in the breeze. It carried the sigil of the First Oracle, a golden dome of rays, a Steer at the helm. As she stared, a sarong of jade green flowed to reveal her slender figure. She wore a crown of solid gold, adorned with spokes to mimic sun's radiance. A tattooed, yet tightly carved face held strong cheek bones and a pointed chin, while ink-black eyes were covered by a shroud of taenite beads.

She turned to face the minister who stood before her, his voice droning at a list of menial concerns: irrigation, guards at the northern gates, design-theft. Each issue met with a subtle nod, her voice bored yet measured, issuing swift, quiet judgment.

Yet Calliope's mind drifted to the flowing bougainvillea that climbed the archways above her. The web she had spun all those years ago, weighed heavy on her shoulders, as did the crown. But the whispers of change were in the air. Patron's hearth was lit, and she could sense the plots being laid before her feet. She had bought her power willingly, poison the weapon used to bring forth her revolution. Control of the sea was essential, and stolen manuscripts told of a metal forged from meteorite that could calm the Veil's storms – taenite.

She manipulated fear of Veil and conspired with her most trusted aids to bring about her own divinity.

Patents were invented, lineage drawn, declaring her the heir to the First Oracle. For the first time in over one hundred years, people found purpose in the Veil's religion and mystery. With taenite strapped to the prow and rudder, quiet study of patterns in the waves gave Calliope the control she desired.

Under her guidance, the Steers claimed piety over the storms, hunting any who dared to test her providence. Regret ached in her chest, the deaths of a thousand men weighing heavily on her heart.

A sudden silence passed over the courtyard, awaking Calliope's senses, her minister paused in their musings.

As Calliope lifted her gaze, the Vizier stepped out into the sunlight.

A purple velvet robe clung to his shoulders, an odd choice, she thought.

"Vizier, does Lysander know you visit me?" she greeted, her voice sharper than usual, clouds, carrying the dark promise of rain started to soar above them.

Ren smiled, the faintest flicker of amusement crossing his lips. He stepped into the light, moving with a gentle grace, as though the path was laid beneath him. "I bring urgent council," he said, bowing his head ever so slightly. "I must speak with you, my Queen."

Calliope's eyes narrowed behind the veil of beads, suspicion tightening its grip. "You may speak in front of my ministers, Ren. There is no one present I do not trust – what are you doing here?"

His smile faltered briefly but recovered quickly. "As you wish." He proclaimed.

The ministers shifted uncomfortably, clearly uneasy at Ren's presence.

Calliope felt the tension rise as the Vizier stepped closer to the terrace.

"The winds are changing, pieces moving into place" he began, his voice considered, deliberate.

"Prince Haru no longer wishes to feed your regime of lies, he works in secret to undermine you."

A chill swept through the courtyard, Calliope's hand tightened. "What do you know of treachery Vizier. Yet how do you know this?"

Ren's eyes glittered with a dark certainty. "I move the pieces, my Queen, I know the truth." He replied, his tone revealing a touch of arrogance.

The ministers glanced nervously at one another, unsure whether to believe the Vizier's words. Calliope's mind raced, questions swirling with the gathering storm. How could he know about the taenite? The overhanging flowers started to twist in her mind, like vines latching to the columns.

Her gaze dropped to the crest on his robe—the coiled worm, a symbol of the old world's most dreaded legends. What power had Ren uncovered? She thought. She had known him for many years, always calculating, manipulative, but this was something else. Something dark.

"Paladin, to me!" Calliope's voice rang out suddenly, startling the ministers.

The Paladin's golden armour glistened in unison as they surrounded the Oracle, leaving Ren and Calliope in a ring of steel. Rain begun to fall, gently at first, then heavier, a fresh scent hung in the air, a light ping echoing off the Paladin armour.

"Speak plainly, Vizier," Calliope said, her tone icy. "What are you saying?"

Ren's thin smile widened. "I hide nothing, my Queen, but bring you fair warning. I have taken residence in the ancient fortress at Patron, the princess of Alkpine is my guest."

Calliope's breath caught, "What of it?" she replied sharply.

"Lysander will come to you asking for passage across the Veil, he is not aligned with my plans. Will you aid him? Or should he seek outside help to cross the Veil?"

"No one crosses the Veil, Ren, not without my say!" she started to shake, "As long as I hold the ore, I hold the power."

Ren stepped closer, he knew her mind, her very fears. His voice dropped to a near whisper. "You think taenite is the only way across the Veil? The First Oracle is returning, Calliope, and when they reach the Veil, your time here will end. I suggest you ready your ships for the Imperator, you will need him for what is to come, the ore will not save you."

Calliope's blood ran cold. "The True Oracle, it cannot be–." The power she had built was a lie, her control was slipping. "So it's blasphemy, the path you've chosen? I will not surrender to your heretic lies" She spat. "I am the true Oracle!"

Ren's expression was composed, a flicker of calm triumph in his eyes. "Perhaps, but heed my words Calliope, your fall is near. The Veilstorm is coming."

His words tormented her, she grew hot, flustered, rain pounded as a heavy downpour swept the marbled courtyard. "SEIZE H-" she fought to be heard against the downpour, but before she could finish, a piercing flash engulfed the terrace, she fell to her knees. He ears ringing, eyes blinded – disarray. The knights surrounded her in the disruption. Finally, she looked up, squinting to see, but like the rain, Ren was gone.

Chapter Fifteen

Guardians of the Veil

The wise ruler knows alliances shift like sand.

Place your faith only in those who earn your trust, for

finding a faithful friend is the rarest victory.

Guardian Throth: The Book of Lore

A thunderous flash rocked the chamber.

Poppy woke in a panic, heart pounding in her chest as the shockwave reverberated through the stone walls, shaking dust from mortar. Something strange had stirred the fortress, the room was heavy, an unseen pressure hanging in the air.

She got up quickly, drifting towards the bare window. The stone was cold, biting at her arm through the light gown as she rested against the sill. The strange light had faded. She wrapped a shawl tightly around her neck and peered out, but the night was black, neither moon showing their face through the rolling clouds above the tower. A brief commotion could be heard, but she couldn't make out the figures shuffling below.

She ran to the door, but the handle would not budge, locked as expected. Poppy remained composed, her fingers rattled at the door until finally, Caladain appeared. His face was tense, his movements quick, she had awoken him from a trance.

"What happened? What was that flash, the shaking?" she demanded, her voice tight with fear.

Caladain pushed the door open, his expression plain. "It was Ren. He's returned."

Poppy blinked, confusion overwhelming her. "Returned? Where did he go?"

Caladain stepped inside, lowering his voice. "Ren has abilities... a power I can't fully explain. He can travel between places... like stepping through the world itself. I don't know how it works, but it's unnatural. I've never understood it, but he comes and goes often, vanishing without a trace, but returning strained, aged."

Poppy stared at him, the pieces did not fit together in her mind. "You don't know how your master moves, yet you still betrayed my father for him? Was it gold?" Her voice trembled with anger. "Why, Caladain?"

He looked away, his hand tightening on the doorframe. "It wasn't for riches... Ren promised power, balance, a place in the history, something... more. But—" he hesitated, guilt clear in his expression. "I didn't know what I was truly getting into."

Before he could say more, a familiar voice interrupted them, chilling the air further.

"Princess," Ren's smooth voice echoed through the hall as he appeared at the end of the corridor, his figure framed by the sharp light of the braziers. He stepped forward with quiet confidence, his presence commanding. "The time is late. There are things you must know."

Caladain stiffened, immediately returning to the stoic guard's stance. The fragile moment they had shared disappeared, crushed by Ren's sudden appearance. Poppy felt her stomach twist in fear, but she hid it, straightening her shoulders, to face Ren's cold gaze.

Ren's eyes lingered on her for a moment, then he turned and gestured down the hallway. "Dress and meet me in the central chamber, Caladain, escort her would you, we wouldn't want her getting…lost."

Ren turned his back, Poppy shot a glance at Caladain, but he would not meet her eyes. Withdrawn in defeat, she went back to dress.

Caladain led her down an echoing staircase, spiralling high up the mountain. The silence between them growing heavy and oppressive. Each step echoed faintly, the long ascent through the fortress an agonizing quiet. She wanted to ask more, to press him, but Caladain's jaw was set, his eyes fixed forward. There was no room for conversation, yet something in his defiance gave her hope.

Poppy had chosen a simple gown that wouldn't drag on the stone floor, soft lilac with a fine broach of silver at her shoulder. She wrapped her shawl tighter around her, but the frigid air gnawed at her, a constant reminder of the strangeness surrounding her. Caladain said nothing but led her through the twisting hall, his face motionless but hands fidgeting. The walls grew damp with condensation, the smell of burning copper stung her nostrils, mixed with a subtle oud of rotten eggs, the combination bitter and repugnant. The braziers cast bright blue and red flames that flickered naturally, reflecting off the walls in a way that made the cavern feel alive and ominous.

The chamber was vast and cavernous, hewn from the heart of the mountain, with the same blue and red glow lighting the space. As soon as Poppy stepped inside, her eyes were drawn to an altar at the centre, adorned with a dark cloth and a random assortment of pewter instruments, etched with more symbols. A sharp dread gripped her, and her heart pounded at the ominous display before her.

She swallowed hard, trying to suppress the rising fear. She had to stay strong.

At the altar stood Ren, speaking in muted tones with an ancient man clad in a tattered purple robe. His face was pale, his skin stretched thin over sharp bones, as though the years had drained every ounce of life from him. The robe matched Ren's, though it appeared as though it hadn't been removed in decades. The old man's whispers were too faint for Poppy to hear.

She moved closer, trying to steady her breath. But her eyes widened as Ren turned toward her, a cold smirk tugging at his lips.

"Princess," Ren said, his voice soft yet filled with authority. "Come forward."

Poppy's gaze flickered between Ren and the old man, dread creeping deeper into her bones. She wanted to run, to escape whatever this was, but her legs refused to move. And then she saw them—three thrones carved into the stone walls, seated in the shadows, almost imperceptible at first. Three ancient figures sat there, silent, and unmoving, their faces gaunt and withered like statues.

Was this Ren's secret? Her blood ran cold.

"These are the Guardians of the Veil," Ren announced, his voice arrogant, filled with confidence. "They have watched over Organon for centuries, assigned by the First Oracle herself. I was chosen as the divine messenger for our time, to ensure the sacred Veil remains... protected."

Poppy's heart raced. She had heard the stories, the myths—but protectors of the Veil? How could this be real? "You're mad," she muttered, more to herself than to them.

The old man stepped forward, his voice gravelly but strong. "The Veil is not a myth, child. It is the sacred barrier that holds our world together. Calliope seeks to tear it apart, but she cannot succeed. You child, are the key to open the Veil - the true Oracle must return."

"No," Poppy whispered, backing away. "Open the Veil! What does that even mean?.."

Ren's eyes flashed with amusement, and his smirk became surreptitious. "You will see, Princess. One way or another." His tone was laced with confidence, as though her resistance was irrelevant.

Poppy's heart raced as her eyes locked on the brazier. With a burst of panic, she dashed forward, her striking the iron base. The brazier tipped, before crashing to the ground, flames pouring out like oil, racing across the alter towards the old man.

He shrieked as the flames spread, and the chamber erupted in chaos and Poppy bolted for the door. Before she could escape, Caladain thrust a strong arm and caught her, ripping her shoal asunder, his grip firm around her nape. Her heart hammered in her chest as she writhed against him, but his hold was unrelenting.

Ren's voice boomed through the cavern, silencing the commotion. "You will open the Veil, child. You cannot escape this place. Caladain, take her back to–reflect."

Caladain led her back through the winding corridors, the weight of Ren's words pressing down on her like a stone. The flames still danced in her mind in a whirl of confusion and dread.

Releasing her, they continued in a berated silence until they reached her room, the tension thicker than clay. The door closed behind her, and she heard the heavy click of the lock turning.

Poppy turned to face the door, her heart still pounding. "What has he become?" she whispered, her voice barely audible through the oak. "You're scared of him, aren't you?"

Caladain hesitated, his face tight with doubt. "He's not the man I once swore fealty to. This power... it's changing him. I don't know what he is anymore, but I know one thing: I can't let him do this to you."

Poppy pressed her face closer, her voice a plea. "Then help me. Help me escape."

She could not see, but for a moment, the mask slipped. His hand lingered on the doorknob, debating whether to open it. A flicker of doubt crossed his face, but it was gone. "I will try," he said quietly, his voice tinged with fear. "I don't know how, but I'll find a way. I swear it."

Chapter Sixteen

Changing Forna

Inner strength is not found at your feet, it is earned through patience, resilience, and integrity – learn to know your true self, to unlock full potential.

Median, King of Trees: Words in the Wood

The sun hung low in the sky, casting long shadows through the rich forest. The canopy above teemed with life, creatures darting in the dappled light between the branches. The air was thick with the sweet scent of ripe fruit as Taro, well-versed in his homeland, moved with ease through the underbrush.

"Here," Taro said, plucking a sun-soaked fruit from a low branch. "Keep your eyes sharp for these; a single one can sustain you for the rest of the day." He tossed one to Berwick, who caught it with a nod of gratitude, sweat glistening on his forehead. His sword now rest across his back, new clothes of leather and cloth hanging neatly off his shoulders, a parting gift from the King of Trees. With

Taro as guide, Berwick began to examine the forest with new eyes. His knowledge of the forest seemed endless— edible plants, game trails, traps— yet there was a subtle shift in the wind that he did not detect, as if the forest itself whispered a silent warning as they pressed on.

The first day of their journey had passed by with little of note. They had travelled hard and fast, stopping only at night to a feast of roasted bush-rat, as crickets lightly chirped around their makeshift camp. The second day began well, but by noon, the forest had twisted. The air grew cold, unnaturally so. The chorus of life vanished, as if the forest held its breath. Sparse trees jutted from the thinning soil, their roots struggling for purchase.

"I don't like this side of Oakston, something feels...wrong," Berwick muttered, his hand gripping the hilt of his sword instinctively.

Taro remained silent for a moment, his eyes scanning the trodden path ahead. "We're nearing the Kreig border," he said, his voice more sombre than before.

"There's something about that place... the forest is too afraid to grow– like the trees know better than to take root."

At the forest edge, the delicate harmony behind them was suddenly replaced by and exposing barren expanse of bare ground and stone ruins. The remnants of crumbling stone walls lying scattered across the landscape, half-buried in the dirt, jutting out like broken teeth.

"This..." Taro said quietly, his eyes darkening as he knelt by a cracked alter. " This was the Battle of Dill," Taro said, his voice low. "When the Veil broke, it ripped us apart. Communities started to fracture, and the elders couldn't agree on the solution – it ended in a brief but violent chaos, and this ere," he pointing to the expanse before them, "is the scar of that tumultuous time. Our last stand against those who had turned… savage."

"Even the Oracle would have been proud, had she not disappeared into the depths! In the end we overwhelmed them–sent 'em north, some say they live on over the mountains, but who knows."

Berwick stood beside him, the weight of history sitting heavy on Taro's shoulders. He could almost feel their spirits, watching over them.

They quietly set up camp beneath the crescent dome of a ruined tower. As the wind howled through the broken stones, they huddled beneath pine-brush, arranged neatly for sleep.

The fire dimmed, unease pressing in from the rustle of trees, even the wind held its breath. Their conversation drifted toward Patron... though Berwick's thoughts remained uneasy. "We rarely leave the forest Wick." Taro said, pulling some meat from a charred squirrel on a stick, "They say wights haunt these northern lands since that war," Taro muttered, his face grim. "I've never seen one, though, only heard whispers."

Berwick's fingers tightened around his sword, the pink-green edge catching the firelight as he loosened it. "My father used to speak of the dead. He always said they walk with us, guiding our steps." He paused, the memory of his father filling his mind.

Taro smiled, a rare moment of warmth coming from the hard-nosed Prince. "He would be proud young Wick. You've got spirit, anyone can see it." The two shared a moment of mutual respect, the bond between them growing stronger.

But the peace was short-lived.

It was the dead of night, and the fire dimmed to a glowing ember. The air turned frigid as shadowy figures crept about the ruins, their movements silent and unnatural. Berwick jolted awake, his heart pounding in his chest. Something moved in the darkness, he could see little of the night, yet glowing eyes glinted around like fireflies – he tossed a heavy log onto the fire, the embers screaming in protest as the shadows paced around him. Their shapes flickered like, barely human, draped in tattered grey rags. Their yellow eyes were hollow and empty, gleaming with malice. Berwick's blood froze as he faced the devil before him, obscured by the darkness. It was a Wight.

A hoarse screech pierced the night as a figure lunged at Berwick. He stumbled, falling into Taro with a cry of alarm.

"Taro, quick!" He bellowed, in the disarray.

"Fire, Wick! Drive 'em back!" Taro startled.

A hoarse screech erupted through the camp as the form lunged for Wick. He stumbled, falling onto Taro who cried out in dismay.

"Fire, Wick! Keep them back" Berwick grabbed the log he had cast into the embers, thrusting it at the creature. Pointed, bony fingers clawed at him, but the spitting flame drew him back. Another fell in behind Taro, the sound penetrating his soul. In a swift pivot, he thrust his axe towards the draping cloak, yet it only caught the air. Berwick's taenite blade glowed faintly in his sheath, radiating outward against the darkness. His father's teachings guided his hand, each swing precise, each strike cutting through the ghostly figures with a boiling hiss. Taro fought alongside him, his axe now alight with flames, until finally the wights were subdued, submitting to the night.

Breathless, Berwick and Taro stood amidst the fading mist, their limbs heavy from the fight. The victory felt fragile, but for now at least, the danger had passed.

"That was close... too close," Taro muttered, still catching his breath. He wiped the sweat from his brow, his hands still trembling as the bitter cold faded. "I don't know what Patron holds, but whatever it is, we'll face it together."

***

The following day, the pair made their way out of the ruins, their path taking them along a stretch of black sand, littered with broken shells and beach worms.

The night felt like a distant dream, no evidence of the wights could be found as they disassembled the camp. In the distance, Patron loomed on the horizon, its tower like a shard against a fog that hung in the sky.

As they approached the bay, the sun cast its light across the gentle ripple of the sea. An armoured woman could be seen patrolling the rope bridge, but it was otherwise deserted. "Water and me, we don't mix," Taro grumbled, kicking a stone into the tide "I don't like the look of that bridge, but I sure ain't setting foot in the water, no matter what. Berwick smiled, "Well, well, seems the mighty Prince Taro fears the water! I never thought I'd see the day."

"Pfft, listen. We need to get over to the island, and I can't see a boat, thinking we draw out that one–" pointing towards the guard "– over to this side of the bay and jump her. All being well that will be all until we can find a way in. How you like being the bait eh?"

"Not very much indeed" Berwick replied, yet the smirk forming on Taro's lip said enough.

They approached slowly, feet sinking into the grainy beach as water from the bay filled their footsteps. The guard was pacing the opposite shore between an archway, the bridge swaying gently with the breeze. From this angle, the stronghold soared high into the cloud, barely be seen against the thick fog that had developed, their clothes wet with the heavy air.

Unannounced, Taro pulled a bow from his belt and cast it out at the woman.

"That'll get her attention, I wager."

She turned, alarmed, and charged towards them. The guard was a hulking figure, eyes locked onto Berwick, drawing fear through his chest. She was filled with a wild frenzy. "Quick!" Berwick announced, he turned, yet Taro was nowhere to be seen. She charged closer, her naked muscles gleaming with grime as her eyes burned with fury. As she reached the shore, a twig snapped, catching her squarely in the jaw. Stumbling, a rope span around her, pulling her to the ground. She tried to escape but the knots that fastened around her, only tightening as she struggled.

"Whaa…" She cried, trashing at Taro who stood triumphant over his catch.

"Well, that wasn't much of a challenge, was it?" Taro said with a smirk.

Berwick stood frozen, baffled by the speed in which his friend moved. The woman was twice Taro's his size, in both height and body, but this was a well-trained agent of the forest, not a sword for hire.

"Crab bait," Taro muttered, dusting off his hands.

They crossed the bridge as the last light of the day faded. A brilliant sheen from the setting sun washed over the water beneath them. Another day's end, yet much still lay ahead.

Chapter Seventeen

On the Warpath

In the silence of true devotion, there is no reason for doubt.

The Oracle: The Book of Lore

Ren landed atop a jagged rise of blackened stone. The portal had drained him, but he stood tall, brushing off the fatigue as he gazed toward the fortress before him, cracks snaking through the dark expanse ahead of him. He stumbled, feeling the strain on his body, before recovering his composure. He dusted off his velvet robe and looked out towards the fortress before him. It was set in the far northern reaches of Umidus, serrated ridges and scorched flats dominated a landscape that had not seen rain for many years. Kreigdeep was built from a rabble of basalt and granite that littered this side of the Valorian Mountains. Before him, a heavy portcullis was shut, barring entry. Within its confines, kept a mass of ravaged people, draped in soiled cloth, and adorned head-to-toe in black markings.

They were the Zealots over five thousand of them, a nomadic tribe prior to the Veil breaking, thriving on the northern reaches' bounty, but in the centuries that passed, had mutated into a contorted and gaunt shape, without the regular promise of sustenance. They were a hardened, broken tribe, their grey skin mottled with detailed patterns bearing the symbols of their people. Crackles and hisses spat from dirt ridden tongues as they writhed towards Ren. Their faith was absolute, and due to be rewarded.

Behind Ren, the elders of Patron watched silently, their veiled faces impassive. The wind howled through the mess of spikes and archways, carrying with it the scent of ash and despair. But Ren's presence here was not one of pity or weakness; it was a call to arms.

He approached the gate with confidence, a larger female standing to greet him. Rhaina looked somewhat bulky despite her cowered stance, a figure as weathered and cold as the land itself. Her eyes were made into slits, a grey-blue shine that pierced the soul. Her face flickered with devotion as he looked upon Ren, waiting for his word.

"The time of her return has come" Ren announced to the hoard. "Will you answer for her on this day? Look to the sky children of the Veil, the Day of Convergence is upon us. The night been blessed once more." As he spoke, Miya became shrouded in darkness, a ring of fire surrounding both moons in perfect union.

A great roar shook the gate, its bars clanging against their chains. "Your piety has been true, unwavering. Now, I ask you to leave this place, take back the land you once called home. Burn those who usurped your people – the True Oracle is with you!"

The jeering continued, louder now as the banging of forced iron clashed in unison. "What are your orders Guardian Ren? What must we do?" Rhaina said, straining to be heard.

"Travel south my child, scorch the earth." He replied. "Raze Oakton to the ground. In ten days, I will appear at the Veil, that is where our fight with the false Oracle will begin."

Rhaina licked her lips, hungry for blood "It will be done, my lord. And she is real? The Oracle has returned?"

"As real as the day she left us the Veil, you do Her work now. She will shine the light before you on the tenth day."

Ren raised his hands to silence the guttural chanting that had begun to echo across the stony plain. The Zealots' voices quieted in reverence as he stepped forward, his eyes sweeping over them.

"My brothers, my sisters," Ren's voice cut through the wind, sharp and commanding. "You have waited long in these broken lands, waiting for her return. And now, the True Oracle calls to you."

The Zealots shifted, their eyes never leaving Ren. Their devotion was absolute.

"For too long, the false oracle in Tifern has deceived the world," Ren continued, his voice gaining momentum, "But we, we who have waited in the shadows, we who have held true to the ancient ways—we are the ones chosen to bring forth the true path."

Ren stepped back towards the line of silent Guardians, who stood vigil over the hoard. A flicker of triumph danced across his face as the gate flew into the air and the masses swam out of the fortress. "Hear me, take your people and march to Oakston. Burn their homes. Show no mercy!"

"It is done then" Ren whispered, turning now to face the elders. The most ancient of the men stepped forward but revealed nothing in his expression. "You have done well, Ren. Very well. Now we just have the matter of the princess – how can you be so sure she will commit when the time comes?"

Ren shifted, unease passing over his eyes for a moment. "She must, she IS the Oracle, and destiny will weave its thread. We have only now to wait."

The Guardians watched now in silence, as more and more grey bodies coursed through the gate, heading towards their inevitable demise.

Chapter Eighteen

The Maw of Sands

Strength and survival are often confused, but true power lies in the precision of intent, not the size of the blade.

Phalanx, First King of Dunes: Truth in the Sand

The Maw of Sands lay deep within the confines of Heurn. It was vast, lit with the golden hues of braziers clinging to every wall. Shadows danced wildly across the irregular shapes of stalagmites and stalactites that gave the space its crude yet spectacular beauty. The sound of jeering resonated through the amphitheatre, as hundreds of spectators tussled for the best view, packed tightly around the central pit. Below, the muffled grunting of the fighting men was barely audible against the cacophony of cheers and groans from the crowd. The smell of sweat and blood mingled with the heat rising from their packed bodies, but Haro, the Prince of Dunes, felt only a cool satisfaction as he watched from above on a platform of stone.

His golden eyes gleamed while he watched the fighters beneath him, their bare, oiled bodies glistening under the flickering light. Muscles taut, they moved like predators—beautifully brutal. It was a spectacle of strategy as much as pure ferocity. The crowd roared as one gained the upper hand, driving his opponent to his knees.

Beside Haro, Ayame sat with a knowing smile, her olive skin glowing in regal radiance. Like Haro, she was dressed with elegance to show her status among the throng below, rich fabrics and glimmering gems covering body. She knelt to whisper something to a man standing nearby, his hood pulled low over his face. The man shifted uncomfortably, casting quick glances toward the prince, while a silent exchange passed between her and the hooded man. A cunning glint crossed her features before she returned her attention to the arena.

The crowd erupted in thunderous cheers as the smaller fighter pinned his rival to the ground, a gleaming dagger held at his throat. The man in the dust struggled, his breathing ragged, bruises and scrapes covering his body.

The slender man had been too quick for the bulk in his grasp, casting blow after blow at his opponent. A wry smile crossed his jaw as he looked up towards Haro, seeking permission to deliver the final blow.

Haro raised a hand from his goblet, a subtle flick from his finger signalling his approval, as he did the crowd hushed to an absolute silence. The fighter raised his blade high as if to strike, but with a quick pirouette, he turned to the prince casting the weapon swiftly towards him. The blow came inches from Haro's nape but before he could recover a roar appeared before him as the assassin, he launched himself toward the prince, a second blade aimed directly at Haro's throat.

The audience gasped in horror, shrieks coming from every angle of the arena, as the assailant moved. Haro's eyes widened in shock, his body instinctively went for his sword, parrying the attack with agility and guile, knocking the man to the floor in shock. The world around Haro slowed to a dazed crawl. He stared at the attacker, guards scrambling to immobilise the attacker. As fast as it had occurred, it was over. Haro's sharp reactions had saved him from certain death. Equally stunned, the larger fighter stood in confusion at the scene unsure where to move.

Haro's expression grew dark, his chest heaving in anger.

"Out!" Haro bellowed, his voice booming through the chamber. "Everyone, OUT!" The crowd quickly began to disperse, the jubilant atmosphere now heavy with tension. Even Ayame stood, her face a mask of fury as she threw one last seething glance at the prince before stalking out of the chamber. Haro noticed her speaking heatedly to the hooded man before they disappeared into the mountain.

Haro remained, his hands still trembled with adrenaline as he gazed at the empty cavern. His thoughts turned to Ayame—who did she run off with? Was she somehow involved in this? The threads of doubt began to weave tightly in his mind, and he cursed himself for not seeing it sooner.

Later, Haro found himself alone in a dimly lit chamber within the heart of his fortress, the familiar scent of burning incense filling the room with bitter smoke. His chest still burned with fury, his hands were clenched, yet his mind was clear.

A woman lay in front of him, still naked from Haro's embrace. She had moved with practiced grace, her hands running over his leg as she soothed the tension from his muscles. Haro leaned back, letting the comfort of her presence wash over him. It was not love, nor even lust, that drove him to her—he needed the release.

Ayame's voice, cold and calm, sliced through the air. "I see I've come at a poor time."

Haro's eyes shot open, his body stiffening as Ayame stepped into the chamber. Her expression was unreadable, but there was a deadly glint in her eyes. Before Haro could speak, Ayame moved towards the bed where he now lay. With a single fluid motion, she unsheathed a small knife from her boddice and, plunged it deep into the woman's chest.

She gasped, blood spilling from her lips as she collapsed to the floor. Haro sprang to his feet, his heart pounding as he stared at his concubine.

"What are you—"

Ayame wiped the blood from the blade, her voice calm and controlled. "Consider this a warning, my prince." She stepped closer, her eyes never leaving his. "You may seek comfort wherever you please, but do not mistake comfort for safety.

Our enemies are everywhere." She leaned in, her voice dropping to a whisper. "And not all of them come at you in plain sight."

Haro's mind raced, the weight of her words pressing down on him. The woman? No, she was well known to the prince. Or was this a threat?

"You think I don't protect you?" Ayame continued, her tone direct and assertive.

"Someone has betrayed you, and with the Oracle's blessing no doubt. This attack is just the beginning."

Haro shifted, her words had worked their magic, how could he not trust her? "Who was that man I spied you leaving with–I didn't see his face?"

"Jealous my prince? How unbecoming of you."

"Answer me, do not test me on this" His voice raising.

Her calming voice soothed the tension that moved between them, "A spy, nothing more. He reports on the goings across the Veil – it appears Lysander has lost his way."

"A spy, well, out with it, what is his report" Haro replied. "And while you're at it, find out who tried to assassinate me!"

"Of course my prince, your will is mine to enact."

Her gentle hand rested on his tight shoulders, easing his stance. She flowed to the doorway, ignorant of the contorted shape of the naked woman she left behind. Blood began to roll towards Haro, a lingering reminder of the cold murder he had witnessed.

Chapter Nineteen

Of Conspiracy

In the shade of ambition, virtue wears many masks. Trust not what is shown, but what remains hidden.

The Oracle: The Book of Lore

Marros adjusted the heavy cloak around his shoulders as he and Ayame slipped through the side gate of the fighting pit. The muffled roar of the crowd behind them lingered in the air, the chants for Haru's name fading as they moved deeper into the quiet tunnels.

"Will he act on it?" Ayame asked, her voice low and sharp.

"He won't," Marros replied smoothly, glancing over his shoulder. The shadows around them held no sign of pursuit, though Haru's calculating gaze from the arena still lingered in his mind. "Not yet."

Ayame scoffed, pulling her veil tighter over her face. "You sound so sure. Haru is many things, but predictable isn't one of them."

Marros didn't respond. Haru's unpredictability was precisely why the prince allowed Marros to walk free tonight, and why Marros' position in this web of lies held steady—for now. But Haru would not expose him. Not yet.

The sand underfoot shifted as they walked, out into the air. When they reached the stables built of wood and cloth, Ayame stopped abruptly and turned to him.

"What will you tell her?"

Marros allowed himself a faint smirk. "The truth, of course."

Ayame narrowed her eyes. "And which truth is that?"

"The one she most wishes to hear," Marros said, his voice light but edged with something darker. "That Haru trusts me implicitly. That you and I are nothing but pawns, manoeuvring to secure her victory. She has no need to doubt me."

Ayame's laugh was dry, almost bitter. "You weave, Marros, but even the finest silk can fray. Be careful not to trip over your own lines."

Marros inclined his head, the smirk fading from his lips. "A lesson I take to heart."

Without another word, Ayame appeared into the shadows. Marros watched her go, the tension in his shoulders easing slightly.

***

The sands stretched endlessly ahead, the Sakana Delta rolling into the distance as Marros urged his horse on. The faint glow of the rising sun cast an eerie light over the dunes he left behind.

Calliope would expect a report, but the ride also gave him time to think.

The assassination attempt in the pit had been a charade, of course. Most knew of it, yet only he bridges the schemes. Ayame's cunning was permitted only by Haru's silent acquiescence. It served his purpose to play the conspirator, to sow doubt and chaos even among his allies. Haru trusted Marros enough to keep him close, but not enough to let his guard down.

And then there was the Oracle. His lover. The woman who commanded faith and fear in equal measure. Marros' allegiance to her was genuine—or so he told himself. But even as he rode toward her summons, he couldn't ignore the flicker of doubt in his mind.

Was it loyalty? Or was it the promise of what she represented—order in a world crumbling into dust?

The wind whipped against his face as he rode on, the warm air running through his hair. His path was clear, for now.

Chapter Twenty

The Weight of Devotion

To love a queen is to walk a blade's edge:

devotion cuts deeper than treason.

Qadi, Scrollmaster to Lysander: Rulers of

Organon

Calliope sat high in a throne wrapped in bronze. She wore a brilliant white gown that flowed endlessly at her feet. Whatever doubts were being spread of her deity, she would at least fit the image of the First Oracle, especially on a day like today. It was The Day of Convergence, an annual celestial festival held now exclusively within the Tiffern capital, celebrating the day Calliope rose to power, and the fall of the First Oracle. Her crown gleamed as shafts of light pierced through slits in the high domed ceiling, illuminating her with omnipotence. Her sharp features were framed by the dark tattoos snaking across her skin, symbols her authority, separating her from the rabble of her court. The great chamber was silent, save for the flickering echo of footsteps as the spy approached her.

The man hesitated before he knelt before the Calliope. He was not used to meeting her so publicly. He pushed back a low hood to reveal his handsome face, marked with a long-curved scar across his cheek. He brushed back his fine mop of golden hair, which had draped loosely over his face. Marros was Calliope's most trusted agent, yet a note of fear struck him as he waited for her to speak. He prayed for warmth but expected anger.

Fresh from the ride, Marros carried the weight of fatigue. He had seen Calliope' temper flare many times and wished to get ahead of the twisted events at the Maw of Sands. He had served the Oracle in many endeavours for almost ten years, supporting her even when she succeeded her father years before. Few knew his identity, and whispers echoed through the hall at his hast approach.

"You failed," Calliope's voice cut through the stillness of the chamber. Her words were pointed, but not yet edged with anger. Her black, veiled eyes watched Marros intently, seeking his explanation.

Marros did not rise, his head still lowered in submission, *she knows – how?*

"The assassin died with honour serving you, my Oracle. He underestimated Haro's instincts, he was quicker than anticipated, I could not risk exposure – but there is one final hope."

Calliope's lips twitched into a thin smile as the cheers outside the palace called for her to join the throng. "Ayame may remain close, but Haro's suspicion will grow. He is not a fool. Soon, he will start to question everything." She leaned forward slightly, her fingers drumming on the arm of her throne. "She must move carefully, yet quickly. I trust you will relay that message."

Marros nodded slowly. "Of course, my Oracle. She knows the risks, perhaps pois–."

"No" Calliope rose, her voice silencing the jeers into an eerie silence. She gracefully stood, arms abreast, her movement fluid as she walks towards the spy. "No, it must be done exactly as I command – no exceptions. Have her do the deed herself if needs be, but it must be public. I cannot be to blame. Much rests of the manner of his death, you know this." Her mind was already shifting to the next problem. "And what of Lysander?"

Marros raised his head to look to his queen. She looked truly magnificent in the vast domed hall, he was struck in awe by her majesty. He allowed a small smile to escape his jaw. "The Reach was a slaughter, my Oracle. His knights never stood a chance. They lay scattered across the rocks. His hope of crossing the Veil without you my Oracle, sits in ruins."

"And what will be his next move? We have cornered him well, but a caged animal never rests." Calliope paused by a brazier, which stood tall before her. Her fingers trailed the flame, as if calling to its power.

Marros, raised to meet Calliope, his voice dropped to a gentle breath, "When I saw his speech, Lysander spoke with resolve, but in defeat, he will retreat to the Citadel—

wounded and cornered. Now would be the time to act, my Oracle."

"Ren's warning rings true, then. Alkpine is vulnerable, and Lysander is desperate." She let the silence hang in the air, her mind weaving through the possibilities. Can I trust those words? Not after he appeared at the High Gardens, not after what he knows. Do I play into his hands?

"Yes," After the pause, "we must use this to our advantage. If Lysander cannot cross the Veil, he will turn back to us, he will not abandon his daughter."

Marros shifted slightly, still kneeling, his voice low but sure. "Do you wish for me to treat with the Imperator?"

Calliope turned her head slightly towards the vaulted ceiling, her dark eyes seeing the flicker of rice and petals floating in the escaping breeze. "Not yet. The time must be right. We will let Lysander wallow in his defeat a little longer. When the moment comes, you will go, but not as a threat. You will offer him hope. Make him believe that, by my grace, he will cross the Veil. But only if he pays homage. He is a proud King, but he must know his place."

Marros bowed his head even lower. "As you command, my Oracle."

Calliope's gaze softened for a moment, the flicker of triumph gleaming behind her veil. "And Marros, do not fail me again."

A twinge of resentment flew over him, she could be gentle, but that was not the woman who stood before him, "Of course, my Oracle."

The spy did not need to be told twice. He rose, disappearing into the shadows as silently as he had come.

The crowd could wait no longer, as Marros slipped away, the Oracle effortlessly floated down the marble steps towards the great palace doors, reaching almost fifty feet above where she stood. She was surrounded by pageantry who appeared without a moment's notice, draped in gold and white to stand at her side. With rehearsed precision, the doors opened without a sound, the roaring of her people erupting through the doorway. She moved to meet them, raising a subtle hand to show her grace. The streets were lined with palm fronds, a sea of green and gold telling of grandeur and spectacle.

As was custom on the Day of Convergence, Calliope took pilgrimage through Tifern City eventually reaching High Garden, where a feast of immense expense was laid out in her honour. This year, it was height of Dampfall, the temperature steadily dropping as Frostrise beckoned. Despite the seasonal humidity, the crowds massed in their thousands, reaching eagerly for her blessing as she moved. Tied fronds of palm and sage covered her path leading through the great city.

Her strength and unity with the people could not be doubted on this day, she was the Oracle, yet fear could not help but creek into her mind as she walked towards her destiny.

Chapter Twenty-one

Lost in Betrayal

Tread not the well-worn path, for it yields no true strength. Choose instead the shrouded road, for through hardship and perseverance, we may conquer the battle that is to come.

Qadi, Scrollmaster to Lysander: The Veil's Whisper

The dying sun, bathed the Citadel with a coppery hue, casting brilliant shadows across the thick stone walls that surrounded it. From the high windows of the keep, Lysander could see far into the distance, the bustle of his city in dire contrast to the bareness that stretched into the horizon.

    The chair beneath him felt colder, harder than before. This was the view he saw before heading down to see off his most elite soldiers, three days prior. He had looked out at his land with ambition, strength, yet now he felt caged and weak of mind. He felt the weight of the crown upon his head, placing it on a desk within reach, a light relief felt as he brushed back his thinning hair. His daughter was lost, now his knights slaughtered.

"My lord, what would you have us do?" Varang muttered, deflated. The crossing at the Reach had been at the commander's own strategy but had yet to feel Lysander's rage at his abstract failure. He approached the window with a cautious step. His voice was worn, with defeated resignation, he had no answer to his King's request for council. "Tiffern's influence is far greater than we expected sire. Yet we cannot submit to her without knowing her true motives." Hoplite finished, his voice stronger, filled with an edge of experience.

Lysander lifted his head slightly, his tired eyes focusing on Hoplite, "And what would you have me do, Scrollmaster? What do the texts say is her next move?" His voice cracked, thick with the grief that sat heavy on his chest. "My daughter..."

The silence that followed was suffocating. Lysander knew the truth—he had failed her.

Another voice broke the stillness. "My lord, we cannot win this fight from a position of weakness." Ryo added, eyes gleaming with cold calculation. "There is one voice she will hear, coin. Our coffers are overflowing sire, but the stocks are full. If we bow now, we may yet gain her favour with say, a charitable donation to her eminence? At the very least it will prevent any further bloodshed – we can ill afford the Steerlanes to close, it may be a small price to pay."

"Will she accept it?" Lysander replied. "Hard to say sire, but it is something at least."

"How–" The Imperator began his reply, yet in a flutter of cloth the spymaster Marros appeared before the Council. Qadi, the Lawmaster, fell back in his chair in the sudden shock, his greatest contribution to the session so far.

"She will accept her own terms, Imperator" Harros announced, his tone strong, confident, despite the glimmer of a guard raising their halberd to his throat.

"What is the meaning of this intrusion? Who dares to disturb my Council..." Lysander paused a moment.

Those eyes, the hood, yes he was the man he caught a glimpse of in the Cenotaph square. But how? "You, he finished, seize him!" He cried, as more gold-plated soldiers appeared at the door.

"I wouldn't if I were you Imperator," his turn was almost mocking, emphasis placed on imperator, as if in jest of his title.

"Explain yourself, who are you that dares to intrude on this most private room." It was Varang this time who stepped up, moving between his King and the intruder.

"I come from the blessing of her most excellent majesty, your Oracle my lord. Here to discuss terms of parlay between our great nations,"

"Your timing couldn't be better" Ryo replied, upbeat in his response.

"Timing!" Lysander screeched, "My daughter is–"

"Yes, yes, we are aware of your predicament, that treacherous snake Ren has crossed our Oracle also. This is what I wish to treat with your grace on."

Lysander's gaze lingered on Marros. He recognized the ambition in the young man's eyes, that sharp hunger for power. It had served Lysander well in times past, but now it felt like a lion-cub prowling at his feet.

Once again, an awkward silence had brewed in the air. All present waiting patiently for the Imperator's reaction. "She murdered my finest men, for what? To drive me to weakness? This is not how you win over allies?"

"That was I, my lord – but of course acting on her great wisdom. Is she not the all-powerful Oracle? Pick your words carefully great King, for she will hear them.

Enraged by the spunk of the intruder, Varang could bare it no longer, "Watch your tone–"

"Varang, enough, he is right of course. We certainly do not accept the blasphemy uttered by Ren and whatever disciples he has converted. Yes, we are with the Oracle… Ryo, draw up the plans with Qadi immediately, and see this… stranger is given the proper comforts of his station, whatever that may be."

Marros lowered his hood once more, hiding his sharp features once more. He knelt before Lysander with a practiced grace that hinted at a deeper manipulation. "I thank you my lord Imperator," he began, his voice smooth as silk. "I thank you, but that will not be necessary, I have the necessary documents here." He pulled a crumpled scroll from beneath his cloak, handing it to Qadi.

Lysander's knuckles whitened as he gripped the arms of his throne. "An offer?" His voice came out low, strained, as if forced through gritted teeth.

Marros looked up, his golden hair catching the dying light. "Alkpine stands at a crossroads. Your forces are weakened, your reach... limited. The Oracle wishes to help. She is prepared to allow your armies passage across the Veil. All she asks in return is your loyalty."

"Loyalty, meaning?" Hoplite spoke with unease. "She demands homage. Do not pretend otherwise, Marros."

Marros' lips curled into a faint smile, his gaze shifting to Varang before returning to Lysander. "Call it what you will. The Oracle offers a hand of peace in exchange for allegiance. Your daughter still lives, Imperator. The Oracle can ensure her safe return... if you align yourself with her."

The words pierced Lysander's heart like a blade. His daughter's face flashed before his eyes—Poppy, held in the hands of a traitor. The weight of choice settled over him like a shroud, he moved to move the crown which sat before him, I pray something of my Imperium is left, when you return my daughter. His thoughts weighed heavy on his mind.

Varang's voice cut through his thoughts, firm and resolute. "My lord, we cannot trust her. The Oracle has deceived us before. Once you bow to her, there is no returning. She will use your daughter as leverage, a leash around your neck."

"And if we refuse?" Qadi interjected, his eyes filled with fear. "If we defy her, we will have no chance to cross the Veil. Our people will remain prisoners within our own walls. Better to align with her now and strike when the time is right."

Lysander's thoughts churned. He was no fool. The Oracle's offer came at a price—his freedom, his pride. But was it a price worth paying to save Poppy? To save his people?

Marros rose to his feet, his eyes locking onto Lysander's. "The Oracle awaits your answer, my lord. Her patience... is not infinite, I return to her at dawn."

Lysander's heart pounded in his chest, and for a long moment, the chamber was filled with nothing but the heavy rhythm of his breathing.

Slowly, the weariness in his eyes began to fade, replaced by something harder—steel, resolve.

"We will accept her offer," Lysander said at last, his voice stronger than it had been in days. "But make no mistake—this is not surrender. We will play the Oracle's fiddle, but we will not be her pawns. I will save my daughter, and when the time comes, I will break her chains."

Marros' smile widened, a cold satisfaction gleaming in his eyes. "As you command, Imperator. I will deliver your message to the Oracle, personally."

As the spy turned to leave, Varang stepped closer to Lysander, his voice low and urgent. "My lord, are you sure of this?"

Lysander stared at the doors as they closed behind Marros, his fists clenched tight. "No, but I will not let her rot in an old ruin."

Chapter Twenty-two

Riding the Waves

"The storm bends even the mightiest tree, but the reed bends further and survives."

Qadi, Scrollmaster to Lysander: Songs of the Imperium

The vessel creaked against the roiling waters of the Veil's edge, a sound like splintering bones. Marros stood at the prow, one hand gripping the railing, the other resting lightly on the hilt of his blade. He stared into the swirling mist ahead, where the ominous shimmer of the Veil's energy danced on the horizon. The usual traders huddled below deck, while the Steer sat at the wheel, whispering prayers to the Oracle, but Marros found no solace in this faith. His survival lay in calculation, not miracles.

As the tempest softened, the Crescent Plains unfurled before him like a golden tapestry, leading to the quiet port of Cyndonia. Cyndonia was a quiet and modest town, famed for its niche trade in furs and leather. The town sat on a flat rise between Barrow and Tifern City, a humble comparison to the grandeur and sheen of the domes and spires of the Oracle's seat of power. Perfect for those with an agency of secrecy and obscurity. Cyndonia thrived in liminality—a place of transit, trade, and discretion. Much like himself.

The journey had been uneventful, giving Marros time to think on the events at the citadel. Marros couldn't help but smirk, weakness was the most valuable currency in the political game, and Lysander had given him plenty to trade.

Then there was Haru. The desert prince played coy with his charming smiles and sly remarks, but Marros saw the ambition burning beneath. Haru believed himself clever, a puppet master orchestrating Calliope's downfall while placating Ren, Ayame, and even Lysander. But cleverness bred hubris, and Marros did not trust him, not completely.

And Calliope...

Marros closed his eyes at the thought of the woman he had grown to long for. The way the steely resolve in her voice commanded the room, and her chambers. Beneath the armour of her title, she was fragile, clinging to her claim as the Oracle's voice even as the tides turned against her. He loved her—of that, he was sure—but love was not enough to tether him. Not when the game demanded adaptability, and the tides shifted faster than ever.

As the ship docked in the steerport, the small crew scrambled to secure the ropes. Marros descended the gangplank with an air of calm, scanning the mid-morning horizon. Cyndonia smelled of salt and earth, its streets blanketed with the whispers of sand and grass seed carried on the wind. The hushed chatter of merchants and mercenaries blended with the rhythmic crash of waves, a melody of quiet deals and a turbulent sea. The Crescent Plains stretched endlessly, a patchwork of golden grasses and whispering winds, where small game darted through the brush and hawks circled overhead.

A well-dressed courier awaited him near the quay, plain in expression and overly rigid for a young boy. He bowed low with practiced grace, extending a roll of parchment marked with Calliope's golden sun. Marros snatched it, stepping aside without a word. He knew its contents well enough: a summons to High Gardens. She was impatience for answers.

He turned towards a tavern at the edge of the open square, with a quickened pace. The Black Coney, swung gently above an open door, the sign faded but still legible. Inside, the room was dimly lit, with smoke hanging in the air. Dust and aged oak dominated the senses. The tavern was a quiet haven for travellers and spies, a place where information was shared in quiet whispers as they broke bread. Marros settled in comfortably at a table near the back, his gaze sweeping the room. A heavyset, mid-aged man sauntered over to his table, a towel draped over one shoulder and grease smothered across his front. He stopped to pour a ruby red liquid into an eagerly waiting cup already placed on the table. He gave a brief curt of recognition, and slowly melted away towards the bar.

Marros knew this place well and wouldn't be bothered. He could reflect, plan his next move in the ever-growing web that surrounded the Veil's hidden power.

Chapter Twenty-three

Veilstorm's Spear

A design hidden in the weave, is only revealed when the final thread is spun.

Guardian Ren, The Book of Lore

The flickering light slowly faded from her window as Ren and the Elders disappeared into the night. Poppy stood motionless in the dim chamber, her heart pounding, still unsure on what this was all about. "How does he do that?" she mused. She sat at the writing desk face in, resignation heavy in her pose, her palms, thoughts dwelling on drifting to her father, her home, and a life `spent watching the world pass from the Citadel's lofty towers. reaching high.

It had been three days in confinement, the time to act was now.

Suddenly, a hand rested on her shoulder. Caladain stood by her side. She jolted, not hearing him enter, but as she turned, she saw a face was set with action and resolve.

"Get your things, we are leaving" he whispered, voice low and urgent. "Quickly—they may not be long."

Poppy looked up at him with a resilient glare and pushing his hand away. "I do not need your help." She claimed, standing abruptly, a look of defiance strong and sharp.

Without waiting for a reply, she darted towards the door. Caladain followed swiftly, drawing a small dagger from his belt as he glanced warily at the dim hallway. "I'm just making sure you don't get caught," he muttered, but Poppy ignored him. "This castle may appear empty and bare, but the walls listen, there is life in its foundations," he finished, calling through the echoing staircase.

The stairs stretched endlessly, shadows bending around each turn. Her breath was fast and deep, adrenaline coursing through her legs to keep her from falling. Each floor she descended felt more precarious than the last, the stone beneath her was slick with seeping moisture seeping from the porous walls.

Reaching a heavy set of oak, carved oak doors, Caladain paused for a moment. "Wait," he whispered. "Narc, she should be patrolling along the bridge, we. We must stay silent".." Not wanting to argue, Poppy gave way to the knight's lead, waiting for his next move. Instead of crossing the doors, he moved lightly towards a low archway to the left. It was dark, out of reach from the braziers that dotted the walls, "It's a dead-end, what is this?" Poppy commanded, but through the darkness, an exposed grate appeared at the floor. "Here," he replied shifting the heavy iron without protest. "I loosened the fixing, we can slip through." "Ugh," she complained, following him all the same.

The short passage cut through the thick fortress walls of the fortress' entrance, a cold gust greeting them as they emerged into the night air. The rope bridge was ahead, she watched Caladain as he stretched his neck towards the bay. Suddenly, a scuffle was heard, followed by sounds of a struggle, "Whaa—" Caladain began, but pushed the princess down and out of sight before she could see what was happening. She peered through the tall grass that clung to the water's edge, the ancient, creaking passage groaning in the breeze. She gazed past the stone statues that loomed over the bridge, the figure as menacing as the worm-like creature she held at bay.

Caladain paused, his hand tightening on his sword hilt. In the distance, two figures approached the bridge. At first, they were barely visible through the fog that had started to settle over the water, but the rustle of their movements gave away their approach.

"They're coming," Caladain muttered, stepping forward with a drawn sword. "Go back, I'll hold them off."

Poppy's eyes flashed with anger. "I don't need protection. You don't even know who they are!" Ignoring his plea, she deserted the brush and stepped towards the statue before her. It towered high over her, but determined to make a stand, she climbed its flank and pulled the taenite spear from the figure's firm grip. The ancient weapon, heavy and cold, fit nicely in her hand, not too bulky or cumbersome, well balanced.

The figures emerged from the mist.

Taro appeared first, short yet imposing, an axe slung over his shoulder. Behind him, Berwick followed, slightly hunched from the weight of his sword and the long journey that had brought them here.

"You're late," Poppy called out, a crude smile breaking the tension as she recognised her promised husband. "We were hoping to sneak you in for a quick bite, but it appears we will have to make do with a bush-meal." She chuckled, speaking with a renewed confidence, letting the weapon drop to her side. Berwick's eyes were weary yet filled awe as he stared across at her beauty, the mace in her hand radiated just as his sword did he felt connected in her presence, stunning him to silence.

"You're late," Poppy called out, a crude smile breaking the tension as she recognised her promised husband. "We were hoping to sneak you in for a quick bite, but it appears we will have to make do with a bush-meal." She chuckled, speaking with a renewed confidence, letting the weapon drop to her side. Berwick's weary eyes filled with awe as he stared at her opulence. The spear in her hand radiated a power just like his sword, connecting them somehow, leaving him speechless.

Taro's gaze shifted to Poppy, lingering longer than usual. His lips twisted into a smirk, though the flicker of awkwardness in his eyes betrayed him. "Princess," he began, bowing with exaggerated formality, "I am overjoyed to see you alive and well, and who is this strapping man? Not a romantic interest I hope.

Poppy's grip on the spear tightened. "From where I stand, prince, that is none of your business. We will discuss the betrothal on my terms," she shot back, her voice cold. "And certainly not here."

Taro raised his hands in mock surrender. "Fair enough, your princess, shall we?" he finished, gesturing back towards the mainland.

Berwick's eyes found Caladain, who still stood tense and ready to fight. "Stand down, friend. We're on the same side."

Caladain hesitated, his mind still heavy with the conflict he fought. He had betrayed Alkpine for Ren's promise of a world cleansed of corruption, only to find himself mired in more of it, but in the end his loyalty to the princess had taken precedence. His gaze flicking between Berwick and Taro. Poppy's sharp voice cut through the tension, her tone laced with command. "You see, Caladain? This is what loyalty looks like. True loyalty, not just blind obedience."

For a moment, Caladain's face hardened, but then he sighed, lowering his sword. "Her words stung, but they struck true. He would earn her trust, even if it meant his life. "As you wish," he muttered, stepping back.

As introductions finished, the four of them gathered on the narrow bridge, discussing their next move. The plan was swift— to reach Barrow, steal a ship, and find a Steer brave enough to guide them across the Veil. Yet as they moved to leave, a distant sound echoed in the wind.

The sound was a deep pulse at first, but the ground started to shake as the noise grew. Suddenly, the deafening blast of war horns reverberated through the bay.

Across the bridge, leaving Patron eagerly behind them, they climbed a ridge and peered out toward the southeast. Poppy's breath caught in her throat as she saw a dark mass marching across the land—an endless tide of grey-skinned figures, clad in crude armour, heavily armed with spears and blades.

"'They're 'eading for Oakston,' Taro muttered, his face pale as ash. 'They'll leave nothing but smoke and ruin.'"

Berwick stared out at the approaching army, his knuckles taught as he reached behind to pull out his sword. "We must stop them."

Poppy, still clutching the spear loosely, felt a surge of cold determination. She could feel the weight of decision resting on her shoulders. "We will stop them. But first Barrow. I must warn my father. I do not believe he has deserted this land, not yet anyway."

With that, they turned away from the ridge, hurrying toward the distant south. The journey would be long and winding to avoid the massing army, but speed was of essence. The wind howled, carrying them forward towards their destination.

Chapter Twenty-four

Letter from Ren to Lysander, Calliope, Haru.

His Most Imperial Majesty Lysander of Alkpine; Her Eminence Calliope, False Oracle of the Veil; and Haru, Prince of Dunes,

Word of your massing legions reaches me, carried on the whispers of the Veil. Your ambition amuses me; like waves upon the shore, you crash endlessly against one another, striving for that which cannot be possessed. As waves return to the tide, so too shall your efforts dissolve into nothing.

Know this: Popelina, daughter of Aridus, moves closer to her destiny. She knows it not, but she carries the key to what lies beyond the Veil—the key to salvation or destruction. Her fate, like yours, is no longer your own.

Already, my army of Zealots marches on Oakston. This is but the first cleansing foretold by the True Oracle. The next, will rid the world of greed and restore faith in the truth. The Oracle has spoken.

As Protector of the Veil, I command you: lay down your arms, or face annihilation. You have deluded yourselves into believing power lies in dominion over one another, yet you fail to see the greater threat that rises with each passing moment.

Still, there is greatness in you, though it will avail you little should you refuse to act. Lysander, no greater leader of men has been born; Calliope, your cunning outpaces any man; Haru, your guile may yet guide you from the path of greed to one of the greatest of riches.

Three days hence, the Veil will open at Barrow. There, all fates will be decided.

Ren, Guardian of the Veil

Chapter Twenty-five

The Charred Throne

Fire knows not mercy, only hunger.

Median, King of Trees – Words in the Wood

The sun dipped below the horizon, casting long shadows over the treeline. A chill settled over Oakston, the first true breath of Frostfall. Rhaina's zealots marched forward, preparing to camp at the forest's edge before breaching its sacred depths.

As the trees stood vigil, their campfires crackled, smoke curled into the misty air. Rhaina sat on the broken remains of a throne amid the twisted ruins at the Kreig border, gnawing on a charred skewer of grass-fox. She observed a heavily marked group chanting the Book of Lore, their faith unwavering despite the broken ruins they camped. Her gaze flicked warily to the darkened forest beyond the firelight. She knew what haunted these parts, her forbears had cursed the land many cycles before but clung to the hope that the zealots' flames would keep the Wights at bay.

She was wrong.

They came silently, their hollow eyes glinting like embers in the shadows. The camp's edge was shrouded in a creeping chill before the first scream ripped through the night. Chaos erupted as the Wights descended, spectral forms tearing through the camp like living shadows.

Panic swept through the edge of the camp, they scattered like frightened deer. Cries pierced the night as the Wights descended, slashing, and tearing with spectral precision. Rhaina leapt to her feet, barking orders, tents were alight, but fire was their weakness.

Torches became weapons, wielded desperately by the crawling zealots who fought the disarray. The battle was fierce and chaotic, but numbers eventually tipped the scales. The zealots drove the Wights back into the shadows, though not without cost.

Dozens lay dead by the dawn, their faces frozen in wild terror. Rhaina's slit-eyes narrowed as she surveyed the scene. Discontent simmered among the ranks, but she stamped it out with brutal efficiency, executing those whose vigilance had failed. Among the grey-skinned zealots, strength was the only currency, and Rhaina could not appear weak.

The rabble pressed onward as first-light took hold, creeping through the forest like spiders through a fragile web. Behind them, they left ruin. Fires burned unchecked, casting dark smoke over the eerie wood. Axes fell against ancient trunks, each stroke tearing through centuries of growth and memory.

Rhaina marched at the forefront, her eyes cold and resolute, a roughly crafted blade in each hand. Each smouldering tree was a victory, each charred glade proof of the zealots' devotion. Oakston's once-vibrant basin was being reduced to ash, the trees' silent mourning a dirge for what was lost.

From the canopy above, Lohith's voice rang out, a sharp cry of resistance. His defenders struck from the shadows, axes and arrows cutting into the zealots' unprotected flanks. They faltered, confusion spreading as they faced an enemy who seemed to vanish into the smoke and leaves.

Lohith moved with purpose, his commands a rallying cry for his people. Their precision was unmatched, each strike calculated, each ambush telling.

But the zealots' numbers were relentless. Wave upon wave of a sea of grey and black surged forward. Flames licked at the trees, consuming all that was sacred.

As the battle reached its apex, the air shifted. A figure emerged from the heart of the burning forest. Median, King of Trees. The frail old man looked radiant and omniscient, the chaos stilled in his presence. Flames receded as he raised his hands, and a wave of force sweeping through the enemy lines, flattening their ranks, and extinguishing the fires.

For a moment, hope glimmered in the eyes of the forestfolk. Suddenly, a bright flash blinded even the King of Trees, a faint glimmer of green piercing the glade as a portal opened. A Guardian emerged, his tall and thin figure cast in their deep purple robes. As the fires roared back to life, he raised a hand, striking Median in the chest with an unworldly force. The King of Trees collapsed into dust, his fading light flickering into ash. "Traitor" veiled on his lips.

Lohith, his heart burning with fury and grief, let out a primal roar as he charged at the Guardian. His axe gleamed, each step fuelled by desperation and defiance. The clash of mortal and divine was brief but ferocious, his blade striking the Guardian as he too dissipated into ash.

The zealots were shaken by as their lord-protector fell and began a hasty retreat. Rhaina ordered them westward, towards Barrow, to regroup and recover their strength for the battles to come.

As the last of the zealots disappeared, Lohith summoned his commander, "find Taro," he said. "He must know of what happened here."

The woman bowed, short locks flecked with ash and dark blood. She left without a word.

From the smouldering ruins of the longhouse, Lohith knelt at his father's throne, now blackened from the smouldering remains, yet it stood whole, protected by some unknown force. As Taro arrived, he knelt at his brother's side. Together, they wept.

Amidst the charred ruins, the foresters gathered, their faces streaked with grief.

Lohith knelt before the blackened throne, its surface warm to the touch yet unmarred by the flames. As the crown was placed upon his head, ash fell like snow, a quiet promise that Oakston would endure—even in desolation..

Chapter Twenty-six

Bloody Council

If denial is like a feast, fear serves the wine.

Median, King of Trees: Words in the Wood

The Sanctum was a place of silent strategy, hidden below the opulent marble walls of the palace. Its sprawling caves jutted over the churning waters below, the relentless roar of waves a constant reminder of the abyss. It was an intimidating place decorated with bare rock and shadow, in great contrast to the opulent beauty on the surface. A council was in sitting, Calliope at its head, with Lysander, fresh from travel opposite. Marros calmly slumped next to the Oracle, indifferent in his stance, with Haru and Ayame sat upright and alert, eyes darting between them.

"False Oracle?" Lysander's voice cut through the chamber like a blade, his tone clipped with disbelief as he thrust the parchment back toward Calliope. "What is the meaning of this?" The chamber was cold despite the midday sun streaming through the narrow windows. The air carried the scents from the Veil below, relentless waves a dull roar in the distance.

The table was of a rich redwood, its polished surface gleaming in the beams of sunlight. Its smooth yet dark surface shimmered faintly in the light. The air was thick with tension, each ruler uneasy with the setting they found themselves in. Haru now took the note from the Imperator and scanned the spiderweb handwriting on the page.

He broke the silence, voice taut with frustration. "This—this drivel is nothing more than a desperate attempt to sow discord." He said, strong in resolve. "Ren believes he can frighten us into submission." Lysander's fingers drummed against the table, betraying his agitation.

Haru leaned back in his chair, the golden embroidery on his robes catching the light. "If steel is what he wants, why bother with this warning?" he said smoothly. "Marching blindly into a goading trap would only hasten our ruin. Regardless of his claims, Ren has some foreknowledge, does he not?" Though his tone was mild,

Haru's sharp gaze betrayed his casual posture. "A trap indeed, my prince," Ayame said, her tone laced with quiet malice. "But tell me, if not now, when?" Haru, suddenly uncomfortable in his resolve, said nothing. Daggers shot across from the Calliope.

Her fingers steepled beneath her chin, the faint beads of her crown catching the sunrays, she turned to Marros who sat patiently beside her. "This army of zealots—what do we know of them?," ignoring the slight, her voice was cold and precise, yet an undercurrent of fear was detected by her lover. "It is not known my queen, the spies say they are a band of wildmen without discipline and measure," he replied. If he reaches Barrow unchallenged, though their numbers would overwhelm us..."

"Enough of this, lies upon lies, Oracle." Ayame stood, taking Marros aback with her sharpness. "Who do you think you speak to? I am not some desert harlot, I am The Oracle!" Calliope snapped, her voice rising in hysteria. "Even now, facing your downfall, you cling to your lies," Ayame said coolly. "You're no Oracle—you killed your father for the Veil's secret and stole his throne." Haru, visible struggling to keep control, let out a sudden and loud outburst, "Enough, it is not your place..." but he didn't finish, Ayame swept across the room, a glint of gold caught Marros' eye, but it was too late. As the concubine launched herself across the room, she pulled a delicately crafted blade from her sarong, aimed at Calliope's throat, an unnatural screech tore through the air as Ayame's blade found its mark. A spray of crimson streaked across the polished table,

   Calliope's body collapsing with a heavy thud, she was dead. Enraged, Haru surged forward, seizing Ayame's arms as Marros lunged without hesitation. His blade sank into her chest, her defiance giving way to stunned silence as she crumpled to the floor. A look of the deepest shock faded slowly from her face as she too sung to the ground in a pool of her own blood. Lysander was awestruck, what chaos had just unfolded? It had all happened so fast. A chair scraped against the stone floor, Haru glanced at Ayame's lifeless form for a fleeting moment, but whatever grief lingered was buried beneath the weight of opportunity as Haru returned to his seat with surprising grace "She pushed too hard" he thought. Marros knelt beside his former lover, caressing her gently. He had pledged himself to her, enamoured by her power and blinded by desire, but his future now hung in the balance.

Haru spoke, his voice strong and deliberate. He turned to Lysander "Your greatness," Haru began, his voice calm and deliberate. "There are truths you must now face. Ayame was a fool—ambitious, reckless, and blind to her limits, but yes, it is true, Calliope was no Oracle. She discovered our secret and used it to control us. Taenite—its built into the ships to calms the Veil's waters. We do not know why, or even how, but we have been trapped in her shackles." Lysander's voice croaked, still finding some composure. "She killed her!" Lysander's voice cracked, wavering between disbelief and fury. "This is madness, Haru. She controlled most of Umidus—what happens now?" a smirk crept across the prince's face, "She did control… Yes, but now, we have a chance to shape the future of Umidus, free from Calliope's lies. Together, we can ensure its strength and stability. What do you say Imperator? "I, I, I must speak with my council, let us summon them. This changes everything. And Ren…" One deity at a time, my lord. "He has taken my daughter." Lysander said softly.

"Perhaps she serves him now?" Haru chuckled softly, the sound low and deliberate, earning him a sharp glare from Lysander, but he spread his hands in mock surrender.

The air in the chamber thickened once more as Lysander's jaw clenched, his pride warring with his anger. Haru watched him closely, then turned to Marros the faint smirk ever playing on his lips. "I can use that one," he thought.

"I will not be goaded by a desert snake," Lysander said sharply, Haru went to raise in protest, but thought better of it. "You are right about one thing," he said finally, "Ren cannot be allowed to reach the Veil." He turned with cool indifference.

"The steers are stretched, and we must keep them maintaining trade routes. Tifern cannot afford to divert soldiers on some crusade. And yet," Haru interjected, "We must act. Ren's letter makes it clear he intends to open the Veil in three days. I cannot say whether there is even a shred of truth in his allegations, but if we do nothing, the consequences will reach far beyond the destruction of the forest."

A tense silence followed as the three-remaining stared at the letter, its words heavy with malice.

"We need information," Marros said finally, raising from Calliope's now rested stance. "I will send an emissary to Ren's army, ostensibly to negotiate. In truth, they will assess his strength and intentions."

"I will dispatch riders to Oakston," Haru offered. "The forestfolk may already be preparing their defences. They could prove useful."

"And what of Barrow?" Lysander asked, his voice quieter now.

"I will go," the Prince of Dunes stood gallantly.

"You have my gratitude, Haru," Lysander replied. "The threads spin endlessly," he muttered, his voice heavy with doubt. "And yet I see no needle, no spindle, and no end.

Chapter Twenty-seven

The Staff

When fire feeds on fear, all that remains is ash.

Phalanx, First King of Dunes: Truth in the Sand

The acrid scent of charred wood and scorched earth twisted in faint curls through the humid mist, lingering beneath a pallid sky. The group moved cautiously by the coastal outskirts of the great forest.

Poppy held the spear tightly, its weight heavy, like an anchor in her grip. Much of the trees lay in desolate ruin, the natural wonder of dense thicket had been reduced to skeletal frames. She looked at the man who had been promised to her, a tear forming against his rough features was in dire contrast to the anger in his eyes. The brittle, blackened stumps were littered with the shapes of birds and animals, lifeless and unnatural, like stones cast randomly into a river.

Poppy's stomach churned, but she held her composure. "This is Ren's army? The army of the man who says I carry the key to salvation?"

Berwick rose, his face unreadable. "This isn't salvation. This is merciless destruction. We walked this path barely a week ago—now all its beauty is lost."

Taro had been silent, his gaze fixed on the ruins " 'ave they reached Oakton?" he thought, wishing the trees could be brought back to life. "These Zealots, these zealots—whatever he's turned them into—this is just..." The poor prince was lost for words as he knelt to grasp the ash at his feet.

They continued through the ruins, the quiet between them filled with unease. Poppy fell back toward Caladain, her steps purposeful as she matched his stride.

"You're quiet," she said, her words carrying an edge. "Did they take your tongue with that dignity?"

Caladain's jaw tightened, but he didn't look at her. "I've no loyalty to Ren. But if you're hoping to goad me, you'll be disappointed."

Poppy smirked faintly. "So, you can talk."

"Enough," Taro snapped, turning to face them both. His usually light-hearted demeanour gone and replaced by something grim. "This isn't the time."

Poppy opened her mouth to respond, but Berwick spoke first. "Tracks," he said, pointing to faint imprints leading east through the ash, "A dozen or so, heading east into the forest. Fresh."

The group gathered around him, studying the faint imprints in the ash.

"Zealots?" Taro asked.

"Probably," Berwick replied. "But they're moving fast" He paused, glancing toward Poppy. "We should follow."

Poppy frowned. "And do what? We are four, they are a thousand, what good can you hope to achieve?"

Berwick stood, brushing his gloves clean. "You're right, and we risk leading them right to you." Poppy's cheeks flushed faintly, unnoticed by Berwick but not by Caladain's sharp gaze.

They set up camp near a beach, a short distance from the ruins, the Lonely Isle just seen poking out of the horizon. A fire crackled softly as day faded fell. A purple light stretched across the dead trees, casting fleeting shadows to fill the site with dread.

Berwick sharpened his blade, the rhythmic scrape breaking the silence. Poppy sat across from him, her gaze distant as she cradled the spear in her lap.

"Why do you carry it if it scares you so much?" Berwick asked finally, breaking the quiet.

Poppy blinked, startled. "I—" She hesitated, glancing down at the weapon. "I don't know. Maybe I think if I hold it long enough, I'll figure out what it means. Or maybe I'm scared to put it down."

Berwick gave a slight nod, his expression softening. "That's the first honest thing I've heard you say since we met."

A faint smile tugged at Poppy's lips. "Don't get used to it."

It was just past midnight when the sound of hooves broke the stillness. Taro was the first to rise, his hand instinctively moving to the axe at his side. A lone rider approached, his horse lathered and wild-eyed from the journey.

"Prince Taro!" the scout called, dismounting unsteadily. "Your father has fallen! Your brother, the King needs you—they are nearing the city."

The words seemed to strike Taro physically, his body stiffening. He stepped forward, his face a mask of shock and guilt. "King?" he whispered softly, "I-I," he signed in disbelief.

The scout nodded grimly. "They're not far now, much is burning. They'll be upon us people in days."

Poppy watched as Taro's hands curled into fists, his shoulders tense with unspoken conflict. He turned, his eyes meeting hers for a fleeting moment before he looked to Berwick and Caladain. "I must go."

Berwick stood, his voice calm but firm. "Go but know we cannot follow." He nodded. "When I reach my father, we will send aid, I promise you," She finished.

Taro hesitated, his resolve faltering as he looked at the scout.

Poppy rose, her voice unexpectedly steady. "Go, Taro. Save your people. I'll be fine."

His lips pressed into a thin line as he looks towards Berwick. They had been through much together, hard to think they met not three weeks prior. With sadness, he mounted the scout's horse. He did not look, but paused before riding, "We'll meet again Wick, farewell for now" he said, though his tone was heavy with doubt.

As the sound of hooves faded into the night, the group sat in silence, the fire casting long shadows that danced against the looming darkness. Berwick watched him go, staring through the night, wondering if he would see his friend again. A hand touched his, Poppy. It was comforting, nice. As she moved, the spear slipped from her lap, clattering against Berwick's father's sword. With a piercing green light, the ancient weapons magnetised towards each other in a moment of unspeakable opulence. Berwick tried to reach his sword but could not, a searing heat reached through his arm, leaving a burn mark across his palm. Poppy looked at him, then the sword, she lent forward to grasp the shining beacon, yet she felt cold as the metal touched her skin "What could this mean?" she wondered, her pulse quickening with the strange rhythm humming from the light. A staff of unspeakable beauty emerged, gnarled like the branch of a tree, its iridescent glow of greens and purples mirrored the fading sunrise from earlier that evening.

"What is this?" Caladain murmured as he moved closer. "Unbelievable... how?"

Poppy looked up to see awe in the knight's face "I don't know, but it is important. I can feel it radiate with my heartbeat, can you hear that sound? Its pulsating from the staff?." Berwick was clutching his wounded hand. "No," he said, he watched with envy as she cradled what remained of his father's blade, yet a flow of acceptance changed his expression, "I don't know what just happened. Maybe Ren was right. Maybe you are chosen—for something. Was all this meant to be?"

Chapter Twenty-eight

Usurper

When the storm rises, all must bow.

The Oracle: The Book of Lore.

Haru stood on the wind-scoured parapets of Barrow, the harbour-city stretched below in uneasy silence. The Steerport lay still, its ships swaying lazily with the tide. Beyond, empty market stalls stood like relics of a forgotten time. The metallic tang of blood lingered in the air, mingling with the salt spray of the sea.

"Prince Haru," a voice called from behind him. He turned to see Captain Ran, his face pale and drawn beneath his ornate helmet. Beside him, the Chief Steer, a stocky man dressed in elegance to hide his sea-weathered skin and a nervous twitch.

"Captain," Haru said, his voice calm but laced with steel. "Steer Constantine. Come closer. We have much to discuss."

The two men approached cautiously, their boots echoing on the wooden floor. Haru's men flanked the parapet, their spears glinting in the sun.

Ban stiffened, standing tall. "My lord, the city has yielded. But we do not serve you, I must protest this incursion. The city will starve with the gates shut. Our reserves—"

A flicker of annoyance flashed in his eyes. "'Protest?" Haru stepped closer, his tone as sharp as his blade. 'I've freed this city from Calliope's chains. The Oracle is dead, her lies and regime are finished."

Ban's jaw tightened. "And in her place, you would starve us? You bring ruin—"

A blade was in Haru's hand before the captain's words could land. A clean, effortless stroke silenced him, and his body dropped to the ground, a pool of blood seeping across the parapet stones.

Constantine stumbled back, his eyes wide with terror. Haru wiped the blade clean on his sleeve, his voice steady as if discussing the weather. 'Any other objections? Silence followed.

Haru's gaze settled on the Steer, his tone softening, though his eyes remained sharp. "Barrow needs its trade. You will continue your work, ensuring the Veil's calm for your ships. In return, the city will be protected, and its future assured. Do you understand?"

The man nodded quickly, his throat bobbing.

"Good," Haru said, sheathing his sword. "The curfew remains. Noone enters without my say. The gates will stay shut." The old man left in a hurry, robes twirling as he went swiftly down the stone steps.

Haru let out a heavy sigh as another approached him from the shadows, Marros, was now dressed in Heurn armour, a far cry from his earlier loyalties. "What now my lord?" he questioned. "We wait, Ren's letter said she will be here any moment, when she does take her to the keep where I can question her. Marros shuffled, our scouts report she's traveling with a soldier and a boy," Marros said, shifting nervously. Haru's expression darkened, his annoyance sharp enough to sting. "Bring them" he said coldly. "They may be useful if the princess refuses to cooperate."

"As you wish my lord. You were right about Ayame, her schemes were poorly executed," Haru looked over Marros, "Yes, you did well in the Maw – your loyalty will not be forgotten."

As sun moved towards the Veil, the city walls grew in stature, shadows moving slowly across the harbour. Haru paced the walls waiting for his prey. At last, a whispered group approached the disorder at the main gate—three figures, creeping around them.

He recognized Poppy immediately.

"Caladain," he murmured, his tone laced with satisfaction. "And who this that boy?"

The guards stationed at the gate glanced up at the tower, awaiting his signal. Haru raised his hand.

"Take them," he said, his voice sharp.

The gates creaked open as Haru watched from above, his soldiers dragged the three forward. Poppy's staff was held tightly in the hands of a guard, the steel searing red under his grip. Her gaze was wary, Berwick struggled against the strength of his captors, while Caladain limped, blood seeping from a spear wound on his side.

"Stand down," one of Haru's guards ordered as more soldiers emerged from the shadows.

"What is this?" Poppy demanded, her voice steady despite the unease in her eyes.

"You're under arrest," the guard said curtly. Caladain cursed under his breath.

Poppy went to bolt toward an alley, but the guard's arm closed around her waist before she could reach it, dragging her back into the fray.

They were taken further into the city. Berwick could not help but recall those last moments with his brother, in what felt like years prior. They were bundled each into their own cell within the confines of the Steersport, plain but for straw on the floor and a bucket to one side.

Haru stepped into the faint light, his smirk a mask of confidence. "Ah, Princess Popelina. You've arrived at last." She straightened, meeting his gaze with defiant eyes, refusing to let him see her fear. "Prince Haru, my father spoke highly of you. It seems his judgment falters with age." Haru's usual smirk formed across his lips, "Indeed" he finished, letting the tension settle. "You may wonder why you are here, we knew of your arrival of course, Ren saw to that, I was sent to collect you of course by your father." Poppy clung to the metal bars that kept her confined, "I doubt this is what he had in mind."

Haru surveyed his captives, when Caladain spoke up "Why, my lord?" Haru turned to him "And Caladain. We have met do you remember? On my last visit to Alkpine, very impressive record. You are here because I wish it so. The Oracle is dead, the Imperator lost in his own failings. Now, it is my time. I will make you, my bride. The Imperator will not stop me. He needs allies. But first, there is the small matter of Ren and his army of Zealots."

Frustration bubbled up inside Poppy, "Why am I always passed around like some prized doll?" she thought. "Bride! I think not, Prince of Dunes. I will not become your pawn." Satisfaction oozed from Haru, indifferent to her repose. "We will see, I think we will remove your friends here and see how that changes your position. He waved a hand, and a small group of soldiers appeared at the door. Caladain and Berwick were both forced out of their cells, Caladain too wounded to fight back, slumped to meet his fate.

Berwick turned to Poppy, his eyes fierce despite the guards restraining him. "This isn't over, Poppy. I'll find a way."

"Oh how sweet…" Haru interjected, "…but ill fated. That staff is quite something. Whatever power it holds, it's mine now—well beyond the reach of a street rat."

Poppy sank to her knees, gripping the cold bars as her hands trembled. Berwick's gaze held hers, steady and unyielding, even as the guards dragged him away. "This isn't over," he whispered.

Chapter Twenty-nine

The Steerport Cells

When the feeble find their strength, the mighty will crumble.

Guardian Throth, The Book of Lore

The cell was worse than Berwick had imagined—far worse than the grim tales he had heard growing up. The air was damp, carrying the sting of mildew and rot. It was a bare and windowless room, no more than six feet square. Only the cold iron bars would keep them both company as they sat huddled in the farthest corner of the room. The faint drip of water could be heard echoing down a dark and endless hallway beyond the bars, which were thick and rusted.

Caladain slumped in the far corner, his head resting against the far wall, slick with a film of decay. His breaths shallow but steady, a fresh scrape on his jaw from the hard rough floor he had landed on. The wound on his side still wept sluggishly, staining his tunic a sweat covered crimson. He hadn't spoken since they were thrown in.

Berwick paced the space, his fingers trailing lightly along the jagged edges of the iron bars. "My brother was in here once," he muttered, more to himself than to Caladain.

The soldier stirred slightly, his eyes cracking open. "What for?"

"Stealing," Berwick said. "He was overconfident, bragging over a recent haul—ended up in this place. Father managed to talk his way out of it, but...." His voice came to an abrupt halt as a guard returned.

"Quiet!' a voice barked from the darkness, but no figure emerged. Footsteps shuffled away, fading into silence.

Berwick crouched near the bars, studying their base where rust had eaten away at the joints. "If we stay here, we'll die. No one's coming for us, no one even knows we are here."

Caladain's gaze hardened. "I failed her," he said, his voice raw. "I swore to protect her after I failed the Imperator. Now she's... trapped."

"You're not dead yet," Berwick said sharply, his hands moving over the bars again. "And she is strong. Stronger than us I'd wager. We'll find a way."

Caladain closed his eyes, his head lolling back again to the wall. "You're mad if you think we're getting out of here."

Berwick didn't answer. He had no interest in arguing with defeat, not when there was work to do. He felt along the bars again, his fingers catching on the crumbling edges of stone where the gate met the floor. His mind raced through half-formed ideas until his hand brushed something cold, damp, and heavy—it was a thick, bloodied stump of wood, discarded but just out of reach outside of the cell.

He grinned. "Caladain," he whispered, turning the makeshift lever in his hands. "I think this might work."

The soldier didn't respond, he just watched in a pitiful silence as Berwick loosened a leather strap about his chest. Carefully, he tied the buckle and threw it towards the stump. "I'll get it…" Berwick said to the stares he received from the injured soldier.

Berwick knelt, his leather strap catching on the third try. With a grunt, he dragged the wood closer—a splintered table leg, stained dark with blood. He grimaced, imagining the poor soul whose blood was on it. He got to work quickly, wedging the wood beneath one of the bars. His hands trembled with the effort as he pressed down, his shoulder straining against the leverage. For a moment, nothing happened. Then, with a faint groan, the iron shifted.

A sudden clang from above froze him solid.

He waited in silence for the guard's boots to thud on the stone steps leading to their cell, but nothing came.

He kept his face slack, his eyes dull. "Help me," he said hoarsely. "Get over here." Caladain groaned heavily but made it to the bars and they moved as one against the lever. The bar shifted just enough for them to squeeze through if Caladain shed his armour. Berwick worked quickly, unbuckling straps, and helping the wounded knight wriggle free before guiding him through the narrow gap.

As they crept through the dark tunnel, a lantern appeared in the foreground. A lone guard. "Quiet," whispered Berwick, as he led Caladain past the archway and further down into the prison block.

A voice suddenly rose, "Who's there?" The pair froze. Caladain groaned in pain. "Wick, that you boy?" The guard appeared, a stocky man with board shoulders and mis-match armour raised a light towards them, "Dase!" Berwick replied, "What are you doing here?" Berwick turned to the man, the lantern's amber glow sending long shadows across his brow, "Been wandering these dungeons for a few moons now, that new pompous prince kept us alive to keep some order. Fortunate I suppose!" Dase shifted the weight only his left, raising a firm hand to Berwick's shoulders. "So that was you we locked up ay? How did you get out of the cells?" Berwick shifted, Caladain looked cautiously at the guard, plotting his next move. Berwick signalling Caladain to ease. "Dase can you help us?" Berwick said, ignoring the question, "we must find the woman we arrived with, please help us?" His calm demeanour suddenly, turned to worry, his face more shadowed, "Ahh, can't be meddling in all that, but look, I won't say a work…never saw you…." "That is something," Berwick replied, he looked at his companion with earnest. "'eard about your father though," Dase replied, "real shame that—good man." The rattle of chains echoed from behind them, someone was coming up the corridor. Dase turned a weary glance towards the noise. "Go" he said, stepping into the darkness, "and good luck."

Following the encounter, they winded onwards through the tunnels. The dungeons was maze corridors and dead ends, but eventually they reached the cells. "Where is she?" Caladain muttered, his arm now in a makeshift tourniquet. "Haru must have moved her further into the Steerport. Wick, let's get out of here. We find Haru, we find Poppy. Can you guide us once we get outside?" Berwick touched the cell bars, "Yes, I think so, let's go."

They continued in silence, creeping slowly through the cold and damp tunnels.

***

Through a final turn, a light began to pour though the darkness. Caladain shielded his eyes, to adjust his vision. "How is it dawn?" he called to Berwick. "Ha, its later than that, full-light at best, we've been down there hours…quick, more guards are coming!" They snuck into an alcove near the doorway, as two gristly looking soldiers marched pass.

They stepped out as they passed, into the middle of the Steerport. The rotunda loomed above them, its bright, curved archways framing the docks below. Soldiers lined the piers, weapons glinting in the sunlight. Not wanting to attract attention, the pair hugged the walls to stay out of sight. Berwick knew the Steerport's layout by heart. He and his brother had snuck in countless times, peddling stolen wares for food and board. He confidently strode, through the winding, empty market stalls, dipping into shadow whenever a guard was nearby. They made timely progress until a formal looking building came into view. "She'll be there,' Berwick said, nodding toward the grand building. "It is the chief Steer's offices, the grandest part of the city. I'd bet my life Haru's taken up residence there."

"Then that is where we must go. Injured or not, I won't rest until the princess is safe." They looked over the building. Doors on the ground were heavily guarded, but two balconies stood empty, that was their way in. This was where Berwick could put his training into action. This was his world, with Caladain by his side, the unlikely pair set up a plan in the sand to rescue the princess.

Chapter Thirty

Letter from Coinmaster Ryo to Haru, Prince of Dunes

His Highness, Prince Haru of the Heurnanon Dunes,

I must express my deepest concern regarding your recent exploits in Barrow, which I fear may be guided by misplaced ambition. While the flow of trade is vital for the prosperity of both nations your recent actions suggest an unwarranted claim on the duties collected by the Tifern steers. Let me remind you that the binding treaty between the Alkpine Imperium and the Tifern Caliphate ensures that all duties levied on goods entering the Walled City of Alkpine remain solely for the benefit of the Tifern treasury. We have received reports of coin departing Barrow for the Heurnanon Dunes—a matter we trust is a misunderstanding. Rest assured, it will be monitored closely.

Furthermore, any encroachment upon the sovereignty or resources of Tifern would have the gravest consequences. The territories of the First Oracle of the Veil, as set forth in the Book of Lore, are absolute. It is therefore my duty to inform you that in the absence of a ruler, His Most Imperious Lysander of Alkpine has assumed regency over the Caliphate, in agreement with the Astra Paladin. The formal process for appointing new government is already underway and will proceed with urgency.

We must also address the matter of Princess Popelina of Alkpine, who I have no doubt remains your foremost priority. Her safe and immediate return to the Imperator must be ensured. As such, and with the impending arrival of the betrayer Ren and his band of zealots, I trust your return to the High Gardens is imminent, so that we may consolidate our forces against this new threat.

I trust this finds you well and we await your swift return.

Ryo, Coinmaster to Lysander of Alkpine

Chapter Thirty-one

Flight to the Veil

A gilded cage is still a cage.

Qadi, Scrollmaster to Lysander, The Veil's Whisper

The room was suffocating in its grandeur. Golden chandeliers hung from an intricately patterned ceiling, while crystal decanters filled with concoctions of deep hues sparkled atop a sideboard laden with untouched delicacies. The bed, an elegant blend of carved oak and silk, loomed in the centre, too perfect to be laid in.

The air smelled of polished wood and perfumed candles, but no amount of finery could disguise the truth—she was a prisoner.

She paused by a large velvet draped window, her gaze fixed on the moonlit harbour below. Minor shone shyly, half-veiled by her larger cousin. The waves of the Veil churned beyond the docks, a rippling expanse of silver and shadow.

A knock at the door broke her thoughts. It opened, and Haru strode in, his robes flowing like liquid gold.

"Still sulking, I see," Haru said, his voice smooth and infuriatingly calm, like steel cutting silk.

Poppy whirled to face him, her eyes blazing. "This place may be dressed in precious gems, and it wouldn't change what it is—a cage."

Haru smirked. "Only a cage until you see reason, child." He stepped closer, his presence filling the room like a storm cloud. "You'll come to understand soon enough. Tifern is mine. Calliope's reign is over. I alone can master her dominion and unite the Hernanon Dunes into an empire unmatched in Organon's history."

"And where do I fit into your empire?" Poppy snapped, her voice sharp.

Haru's smile widened. "You'll be its jewel, of course. Its future. We'll wed, and your father will yield to save you—his precious daughter. Together, we'll secure an heir, and your name will be spoken with reverence for generations."

Poppy's hand tightened as she stepped back from the window ledge. "You're delusional if you think I'd ever agree to that."

"Agree?" Haru chuckled darkly. "You misunderstand, Princess. This is not a request." He withdrew a folded letter from his robes and tossed it onto the bed. "Your father is lost. Read this if you doubt me."

Her anger flared. Ignoring the letter, she swung at Haru with a clenched first, landing a solid blow against his cheek with a satisfying thud.

He staggered back, his smirk vanishing as his eyes darkened with fury. "You'll regret that," he hissed, his voice low and venomous.

He strode to the door, staining the golden rug as he spat out blood from the blow. He left the room, pride stinging, and slammed it in the face of the guard waiting outside.

**

Some time later, as Miya began her waxing fall towards the horizon, the door reopened to reveal frail, nervous-looking man. His stooped posture and lined face spoke of weariness, but his sharp, calculating eyes betrayed a sharp mind.

"Constantine, I presume," Poppy said coolly.

The Chief Steer inclined his head. "Your Highness," he said, his voice steady despite the tension in his frame.

"You're not here of your own will," she said, studying him. "Haru controls the city, doesn't he?"

Constantine hesitated, his gaze darting to the door. "Barrow is... under duress. The Steers are loyal, but my position is precarious."

Poppy stepped closer, her tone softening. "Then help me. You've lost control of the harbour, but you could yet regain it. Haru's tyranny will destroy Tifern. You know that as well as I do."

Constantine's hands trembled slightly. "What can I do, Your Highness? I have no army, no allies, all we know is the Oracle."

"Arrange passage, get me out of this place" Poppy said firmly. "Into the Veil, only death waits for me here. I need to reach my father."

The Steer's gaze searched hers, his expression torn. Finally, he nodded. "I'll make the arrangements, but I cannot guarantee your safety past this door."

He turned to leave, looking round as he held the handle. "Oh and Princess, the Prince of Dunes wishes for your presence tomorrow morning – he has some event planned… he would hate for you to miss it."

***

The hours passed slowly, as Poppy waited in earnest. She watched as the dock bustled despite the patrolling guards who walked slowly across the web of boardwalks. At last, a faint knock wrapped at the door.

Constantine entered, his face pale but determined. "It's time," he said. "Follow me."

Poppy followed him through the door, a soldier lay in a hump on the carpeted hallway. She stepped over him, watching as the Steer adjusted a portrait on the opposite wall to reveal hidden passage. The passage was narrow, the muffled sound of voices could be heard above them, dust falling through creaking floorboards and feet shuffled.

Constantine's breathing was shallow as he paused to check the path ahead. They moved silently and swiftly through winding corridors, pausing only to light a candle to light the way. They emerged at a private dock at the base of the rotunda where a mid-sized boat bobbed gently in the water. A lone Steer waited them, weathered hands resting on the tiller.

The boat's hull gleamed faintly in the candlelight, the inlaid taenite reflecting vividly into the water. Poppy ran her fingers along the smooth metal, feeling the faint, pulsing breath beneath her fingertips—a calming resonance that seemed to echo in her chest.

"It calms the waters, not through divinity, but science" Constantine said quietly. "This precious metal is how our ships cross through the steerlanes. Without it, the Veil would consume us. The Orac… Calliope, told many lies to claim regency over Umidus, this I believe was eventually her downfall. I fear the day when the true Oracle returns to us and unleashes the storm within."

Poppy nodded, her gaze lingering on the horizon. The boat rocked as she climbed aboard, the Steer already preparing to push off.

Suddenly, shouts rang out behind them. Poppy turned to see Berwick and Caladain sprinting toward the docks, her staff in the boy's hand, with soldiers in pursuit.

"Go!" Berwick shouted, his voice hoarse.

Caladain staggered, an arrow was buried deep in his thigh. He shoved Berwick forward, his movements desperate, before the weight of a launching soldier took him to the ground."

Berwick leapt onto the boat as it pulled away, his chest heaving. "We can't leave him!"

"We have no choice," Poppy said, her voice breaking as the cries of battle rose behind them.

The bells of war sang through the harbour, their echoes swallowed-up by the roar of flames and the clash of steel. From the ship, Poppy could see the first fires rise as

Ren's zealots breached the gates, succumbing Barrow to his chaos."

Poppy gripped the edge of the boat as they launched into the night, her knuckles white as the Veil's waters stretched before them. Behind her, Barrow descended into chaos, a city lost to fire and sword. Caladain was gone.

Berwick sat beside her, still clutching the metal staff, deep in thought. He lookup and raised it to her in gentle submission. She noticed his eyes, kind and warming to her heart, as if speaking in an unspoken language of mutual understanding. He handed it to her without a word as she intertwined her arm in his, resting her head on his shoulder. So much had been lost, but they had each other at least.

Chapter Thirty-two

The Battle for Barrow

Fortune smiles upon the wicked as much as the just yet leaves both unfulfilled when the heart falters.

Phalanx, First King of Dunes, Truth in the Sand

Haru left the princess and returned to the parapets, his frustration with her showing through his angry strides and he sped towards the city walls. As the sun set, hues of red and gold caught the rolling clouds that formed on the horizon, casting a heavy glow over the city. With it, the air became thick with moisture, an unusual cold and clammy chill swept through his bones.

As he reached the stairs leading above the city gates, he observed his forces below. They were well drilled and stood proudly in the golden cloaks synonymous of Heurnanon. Their armour gleaming faintly in the muting light.

A horn rang out, calling his attention to beyond the gates, chaos was coming.

The zealots had filed into the landscape, their line stretching far out into the smoky remains of Oakston in the far distance. They moved like a tide, dirty, unkempt faces garbed in mismatched armour and animal pelts. Despite the disorder among their ranks, they paused to surround the gates where Haru stood, with one among them stepping forward to meet his gaze.

She did not speak but held aloft the head of one Marros' man, sent to scout the hoard. It was not a fresh cut, tar stuck to the base to keep it from rotting. The leader threw it casually to the ground, like discarding a bone at a feast having eaten your fill. She smiled, revealing rows of sharpened yellow teeth which drew fear into the men who stood vigilant.

Not a word passed between them, but as if drawn by some distant signal, the mob surged forward in a disjointed wave. War cries carried through the stillness, chilling and primal. They bore no siege engines, but fire arrows arced overhead, slamming into roofs and market stalls, sending plumes of green acrid smoke into the sky.

"They'll burn the city before they break the gates," Haru muttered. His voice was steady, but gaze filled with steel.

"Prince Haru!" a soldier called from behind him, saluting sharply. "The eastern quarter is alight. Shall we send troops to put out the fires?"

"No," Haru said coldly, his eyes never leaving the rabble below "Many will die this day," he thought. "They'll spread themselves thin soon enough. Focus all forces on the gates. Archers!"

Another bell rang out, echoing across the stone walls. Lines of archers moved in unison, to the drumbeat playing from a tower near the gates. The whistle of arrows filled the air, cutting down scores of zealots at the front line, yet more poured forward, stepping over the bodies of their fallen with reckless abandon.

Haru surveyed the battlefield with a practiced eye. Though disorganised, the sheer numbers of the zealots posed a real threat. His troops were holding—for now—but he could see the cracks beginning to form.

"Hold the line!" he barked, his voice cutting through the din of war. Soldiers rallied at his command, forming tighter ranks above the gate. Hidden amid the mass of bodies that swarmed forward, a wooden ram rolled towards the gate.

"Ram!" a page cried, dropping the bundle of arrows he held.

A thunderous crash ripped through the city, the wooden gates splintered. The zealots surged through the opening, a feral horde descended on an organised line of Haru's forces lances.

"My lord, the gates have fallen!" A young officer stumbled to Haru's side, his face pale. "I can see that, you fool—," but before he could respond another runner arrived, panting and wide-eyed. "Your Highness," the soldier gasped, "the princess—she's escaped. The Steer dock—she's gone! We have the knight, but the boy escaped too."

The news hit Haru like a hammer. His jaw clenched, his knuckles white around his sword hilt. "Damn her," he growled under his breath. "Damn them all."

Turning back to the fray, Haru's face hardened as he saw the breach. "Keep a vigilant watch, I will question him later" he snapped at his officer.

Without hesitation, he descended from the parapets, plunging into the mass of grey bodies and gold cloaks. His blade flashed in the smoky haze, cutting through the zealots with calculated precision. He moved with a commander's focus, every strike a rallying cry for his troops. Around him, his men fought with renewed fervour, emboldened by his presence.

Despite his efforts, the tide of battle seemed poised to overwhelm them when a new sound rose above the cacophony—the thunder of hooves.

From the edge of the broken woods, a small but disciplined cavalry force sped towards them. At their head rode two men: Taro and his brother Lohith of Oakston. Their steeds were unlike any seen in Barrow—blueish pearl in colour with light grey spots along their hindquarters, their maneless heads compact yet strong. Their hooves rang out in unison, a melodic rhythm against the chaos of battle.

The mounted soldiers charged into the zealots, a mix of spears and axes tearing through the rabble like a knife through butter. Taro's axe swung with lethal efficiency, while Lohith's sword danced with grace. The sight of the cavalry broke the zealots' momentum, scattering their lines and giving Haru's forces the reprieve they desperately needed.

The battlefield fell into a tense quiet as the last of the zealots fled into the mist. In the distance, a strong flash illuminated the battlefield. Haru turned towards it to see a man disappearing into its light.

He moved to meet the men approaching the shattered gates. Taro dismounted, his armour spattered with blood and grime, Lohith joined him with a grim expression across his face.

Haru approached them, his own tunic torn, and face streaked with dirt. "You're here," he said curtly, his tone carrying a hint of bitterness.

"We came as soon as we could," Taro replied, his voice heavy. "We pushed them back at Oakston, one of their Guardian is dead. Struck down in the madness of battle. His body turned to dust." Lohith said, he took a breath, regaining composure from the battle. "Where's the princess? And Wick, are they safe?" finished Taro.

Haru's expression tightened. "The princess has gone," he lied. "She sails to her father under my protection."

Taro's brow furrowed. "Gone? I missed her."

"There was no time," Haru said sharply. "Barrow was burning, and Ren's forces were at the gate. She's—safe—that's all that matters."

Taro exchanged a glance with Lohith, his unease evident. But before he could press further, Haru turned to his officers.

"Your assistance has been noted, but you are dismissed." he ordered. "Barrow is no longer your concern. Return to your forest—I have no need of outsiders meddling in my city."

Taro stiffened at the dismissal but said nothing. As he and Lohith left the gates, the two brothers fell into a hushed conversation.

"He's lying," Lohith said, his voice low.

"I know," Taro replied. "Something's wrong here. I'll stay tonight, under cover, but withdraw to the treeline and set up camp. I'll see what he's hiding."

As the brothers parted, Haru ascended the parapets once more, his gaze fixed on the smouldering battlefield. In the distance, he looked towards where he had seen the flash. "Ren," he thought, pausing to reflect on what it meant.

Haru's grip tightened on his sword. His first test was over, but there would be more to come.

Chapter Thirty-three

Oracle of the Veil

To navigate the unknown, one must first become

it.

The Oracle: The Book of Lore

The boat creaked against the churning waves, salt spray stinging Berwick's face as he clung tightly to the prow. Smoke still billowed from Barrow, but was fading into the horizon as dawn signalled the first light of day. The air was thick as mist began to gather on the water's surface, like a net waiting to engulf the vessel.

The sea around them was restless yet dulled somehow underneath them. They gently crested each wave as if guided by the storm. Berwick glanced towards the Steer, who gripped the tiller with practiced ease. He was calm, weathered, and unmoving. A part of the boat rather than its pilot.

"How often do you cross?" Berwick asked, his voice raised over the crashing foam.

"Every moon I've lived through," the Steer replied without turning. "The steerlanes are charted by tides and currents. Once you learn their flow, they guide you true."

Berwick frowned. "And the beast that lurks in its depths? The one from the stories?" The Steer let out a dry laugh, his eyes fixed on the horizon. "Tales for children, my boy. No sea serpent has ever shown its face in my lifetime, only the Veil's temper to fear. Stay the course, and we will be safe."

Berwick leaned back. A wreck rested in the middle distance—a galley of the finest cedar, now stained and splintered, weathered against a crest of rock. "A fair warning that," the steer said – "never go against the Veil, she will take you like any other." He let the words settle. Berwick had never crossed the Veil. The endless expanse of water was both alluring and intimidating.

"Do you always believe every story you're told?" Poppy's voice cut through his thoughts, sharp with amusement. She sat across from him, her back straight and chin high.

He turned, a faint grin meeting hers. "Not every story, Princess, but enough to keep me cautious."

"Well, I've crossed the Veil several times," she said, tossing her hair back, "and I've yet to see the beast that concerns you. Waves, wind, and a terribly upset stomach. Nothing more."

Berwick chuckled, though the motion of the boat was starting to take its toll.

Poppy hesitated, then shifted closer. "Breathe deeply, Wick," she said, placing her hand on his shoulder. "Wick?" he asked, the faintest blush creeping up his neck.

Her cheeks coloured too. "If you prefer Berwick?" she muttered. "No, Wick is nice… Poppy." His smile caught hers once more. "It'll pass, you get used to it. Do you know the full story? Of Elysian and Prypat?" She said, returning her hand. "Prypat, no?" Berwick replied. "There were once two great cities in Organon, each competing for dominance and affluence. Elysian was the Oracle's jewel. A thriving civilisation of beautiful architecture, achedemia and opulence. It is said that the Oracle herself lived at its heart, a beacon of hope in an early world. Prypat, however was its antithesis. A hive for villainy and deceit, home to non-believers. Over time, however, borders blurred and the two formed a symbiosis, becoming dependant on each other through trade culture. As the two peoples met, faith in the one Oracle began to slowly fade until on the Day of Convergence, they revolted with one voice. In her defence, the Oracle called upon the source of her power, the Veilstorm, which rose up to destroy both people without prejudice. The beast tore Organon in two and the Veil we know today filled the void, but deep beneath the waves, the ruins of those cities wait endlessly for her return, endlessly begging for forgiveness, even calling to her through the waves. A tale to inspire loyalty no doubt, but nothing more…"

The Steer called out, "Sects Ahead!" Both Berwick and Poppy sat in sudden silence.

***

Three islands came into view, rocky and barren, their surfaces rising from the restless waves like a defiant child. The waters surrounding them were choppy, crashing against the rocks with relentless fear, yet, as the boat neared, they glided through the tumult as if carried by some unseen hand.

Berwick's eyes narrowed. A figure stood on the largest of the islands, silhouetted against the grey sky. "Someone's there," he said, pointing.

Poppy followed his gaze, her stomach sinking as she recognised the figure's dark robes. "Ren," she whispered, her voice tight with dread.

The Steer waved dismissively. "Passersby, likely. We'll stay our course." But as the boat approached, the figure's arms raised. The staff began to vibrate violently, they shifted to watch it erupt with green and purple from its core.

"What—what's happening?" Poppy gasped, grabbing the staff.

As she did, the Veil's waters roared to life, colossal waves encased the boat in a shimmering, iridescent dome. The world became silent save for the low hum of the staff.

"Drop it!" Berwick shouted, panic flashing in his eyes.

Poppy's hands burned, the heat searing through her gloves. She let go, the staff piercing the boat's hull with a sickening roar. Water rushed in, the boat groaning under the weight of its wounds, the protective dome fell, sending the Veil crashing into the boat.

The next moments were chaos. The boat splintered, throwing them into the icy grip of the Veil. Berwick reached for Poppy, but she tore free, diving into the depths.

The water was black and endless, the staff's glow their only light, it drew her deeper. Her hands desperately reach for it, her lungs burning for air.

Berwick didn't see what happened next, but the world shifted. The sea split, Berwick coughed and sputtered as he found himself on sandy ground. Waves towered above him like a wall, fish darting in the eerie light.

Poppy stood in the centre, a bed of vibrant green seaweed under her feet. The staff held tightly in her grasp, its glow enveloping her in an otherworldly light.

"Poppy?" Berwick whispered, his voice trembling with awe.

She turned to him, her expression unreadable. "Wick, I saw something, someone... We have to move," she said, her voice steady but distant.

Together, they rushed along the coral path, the water parting before them in deference. The bank rose steadily, leading to the rocky lip of the island head where she knew Ren waited.

He stood tall, his black robes flowing unnaturally in the still breeze. As they approached, he lowered his gaze and fell to one knee.

"Princess Popelina," he intoned, his voice reverent. "The Oracle returns."

"Your wrong Ren. So very wrong – I have seen it." She replied.

"I too have visions, Princess, and its coming." He looked up to her, his gaze filled with an awe never seen before on the former Vizer.

"Whatever the path, I serve you–"

Poppy's knuckles whitened around the staff. Without hesitation, she swung it in a brutal arc, striking Ren's temple. A final smirk swept across his wiry face. Before Wick could react, he dissipated into the wind, carried into the Veil as the waves fell heavily behind her. Only his emerald trinket remained.

Chapter Thirty-five

Epilogue

Peace, like darkness, waits for vigilance to falter. Those who deny it are safe in their ignorance, until the hammer falls once more.

The Oracle: The Book of Lore

Barrow's streets still smouldered as the news of Calliope's death and the Veil's stirrings swept through Tifern. These whispers quickly turned to a blind panic among the peoples of this fractured land. False or not, the Oracle was gone. Her lies had been exposed, and with it, the fragile threads that bound Tifern and Umidus began to fray. In the chaos, Haru moved swiftly, his golden cloak now a mantle of command. He placed loyalists on the Steer's ships, watching for the slightest act of defiance. To the people of Tifern, he promised stability, in return for order, and imposed a vast number of laws restricting their movements and freedoms. Behind closed doors, he crushed dissent, silencing those who dared to question him.

In the shadows, Taro worked against him. Finding the truth of Poppy's escape, he acted on rage, fearing the worst. He struck from the unseen corners of the Caliphate, leading a resistance of what remained of his own people. He was fuelled by anger, mired with guilt, with rumours of his defiance spreading from the Reach to the Razors, his name whispered with hope among those who resented Haru's iron hand. Each of Taro's calculated strikes weakened Haru's grip—small acts of rebellion, but enough to sow doubt and mistrust within his ranks.

In High Gardens, Lysander sat watching in quiet contemplation from his clifftop refuge, as the Veil stirred ever more violently, his gaze fixed on the sea for signs of his daughter. In a move that shocked his council, he broke from his mourning to move in open defiance against Haru, joining Taro's rebellion, seeking solace in his newfound isolation.

The loss of Calliope and the rise of Haru weighed heavily on him, but it was the Veil that consumed his thoughts. Perhaps Ren was right, was there more to his daughter than he had realised? She was far from his reach, yet closer to the heart of this chaos than ever before. What role would she play in the storm to come? Could she wield this ancient force, or would it consume her?

His hand drifted to his sword, the seal of Alkpine set into the handle. Returning to his Imperium seemed impossible now; too much was at stake here. Yet to stay and resist Haru's growing dominion might cost him everything.

The quiet rumble from the courtyard grew ever louder, the distant roar of the Veil's voice growing louder with each passing day.

Far from the towering cliffs at High Gardens, Poppy and Berwick drifted further into the void, heading for a strange calling that she alone could hear. They took the boat Ren had left moored on the island, her staff rested across her lap, its faint green and purple glow pulsing like a heartbeat. The waters surrounding them were restless, as though something ancient and terrible stirred within it.

Berwick watched her carefully, his hand caressing hers in quiet reassurance.

Though he said nothing, she felt the weight of his presence—a grounding force amid the chaos.

"It's alive. I can feel it stirring beneath us...something vast, something waiting."

Berwick didn't reply. He had no answers, only questions. Together, they would have to navigate this strange and dangerous path—balancing her growing power against the chaos rising in Organon.

As the boat crested another wave, Poppy tightened her grip on the staff. In the distance, the faint outline of land emerged from the mist—a promise of sanctuary or danger, she couldn't yet tell, but jagged, foreboding peaks formed as they neared.

The Veil whispered around them, its voice rising like a distant chorus. The storm within it—and within her—continued to grow.

Appendices

Appendix A

Light Phases

Light Phase	Timing	Meaning
Dawn	Sunrise to mid-morning	Balance and reflection
Full Light	Late morning to mid-afternoon.	Work and energy peak.
Waning Light	Late afternoon	Transition and rest.
Twilight	Sunset and Moonrise	Endings and change.
Deepnight	Night and Moonset	Secrecy and shadow.
Starfall	Latest night	Celestial renewal

Appendix B

Dayturns

Dayturn	Order
Orturn	1
Lunturn	2

Diturn	3
Penturn	4
Vunturn	5
Celturn	6

Appendix C

Seasons

Name	Meaning
Vernal	Growth, the awakening of life.
Scorch	Heat, trials and perseverance.
Dampfall	Transformation, cleansing, preparation.
Frostrise	Cooling, rest, reflection.

Appendix D

Units of Time

Unit	Description	Collective	Notes
Light Phase	Smallest unit of time, six per dayturn	Six per dayturn.	Length varies by Season
Dayturn	A full Organon rotation		Organon day structure
Miya Phase	Luna week structure	Six Dayturns	Luna week structure
Miya Cycle	A full Miya rotation	Eighteen dayturns, or three Miya phases	Luna month structure

Minor Cycle	A full Minor rotation	Twenty-four dayturns, or four Miya phases	Second lunar month structure
Season	The four phases of solar rotation	Sixty dayturns, or three Miya Cycles	Full weather phase
Full Cycle	A full solar rotation	Two-hundred and forty dayturns or four seasons	Solar year structure

Appendix E

Map of Organon

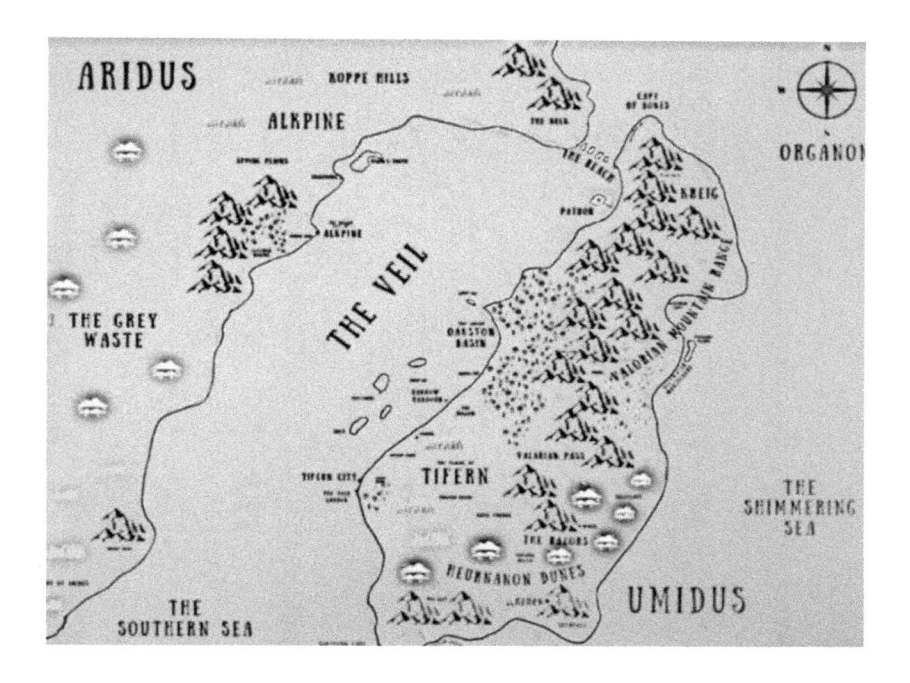

Appendix F:

Annulum Alphabet